THE SORROW AND THE SEA

FATED: POSEIDON AND AMPHITRITE

OTHER BOOKS

Fated

The Head and the Heart

The Flower and the Flame

The Sorrow and the Sea

Cursed

The Princess and the Prophecy

The Fallow and the Faint

The Weaver and the Web

THE SORROW AND THE SEA

FATED: POSEIDON AND AMPHITRITE

KERRI KEBERLY

The Sorrow and the Sea
Copyright © 2024 by Kerri Keberly

Cover design by Keith Robinson

Dragonfire Press

Print ISBN: 978-1-958354-72-8

CHAPTER 1

Amphitrite belonged to the sea. Not only because she was one of fifty daughters of the sea gods Nereus and Doris, but because she so lovingly cared for the life that dwelled within its watery depths.

She swam with purpose, on her way to a reef and its colorful residents she visited often. When she reached her destination, she stopped and admired the urchin and anemone, humming soothingly as she did. She moved along the reef, calling for the old turtle that lived there to come out of its shell. It was an ancient language, the sound more akin to singing than actual words.

She bit her lip, worried when her friend did not stir from its usual spot within the coral. She moved closer, peering into a dark crevice and calling for it again, louder this time. Just as her worry bordered on panic, it appeared, popping its head out of its hiding place.

"There you are," she said, breathing a sigh of relief before running her forefinger over the top of its head.

She was kind to all creatures, whether they possessed fin or claw, shell or scale, and though she could not explain it, felt compelled to look after them, even the fearsome sharp-toothed and powerful tentacled creatures.

Amphitrite didn't know why it was her nature to offer comfort to the inhabitants of the ocean, it just was. And so, she would swim from reef to reef, gliding along the frigid depths before rising to the shallow tide pools warmed by the sun, to make sure all was well, especially after a violent storm had rolled and thrashed the waves.

A small shudder rippled through her. She knew of the Olympian who had been given rule over the oceans by Zeus, as all who lived under the water did. He was called Poseidon, and when he raged, so did the sea. He was disgruntled quite often, and she wondered what made him so. Her father, Nereus, was always so even tempered. Nothing seemed to shake him. Perhaps it was because he was a Titan, an old god responsible for only a small part of the sea. To her, his domain seemed vast, but it must be small in comparison to King Poseidon's.

Poseidon ruled over the entirety of the sea, and every ocean, big and small, across the world. Amphitrite could not imagine what that would be like, to have such great responsibility. With so much power, was it any wonder he lost his temper sometimes?

For all the days the sea was rough, there were also many days it was calm. It was beautiful when it was the latter, making living under the waves a joy and delight. During these times of peace and tranquility, Amphitrite enjoyed the company of her many sisters, though some, she must confess, more than others.

The twins Galene and Galatea were her favorite, born close in age to Amphitrite. Galene could be bumbling at times, but in general, always seemed quite happy and optimistic. Amphitrite found she could speak to Galene about anything.

Galatea was much the same, but lately she had been spending all her time ashore. Amphitrite had heard a rumor Galatea was in love with a mortal man, but she didn't believe it. Perhaps Galatea had stumbled upon him in need of help, or he could have offered her assistance in some way. Her sisters loved to gossip. Something Amphitrite never much cared to do. Galatea had made a friend and nothing more. Why else would a nereid bother herself with the world above? Everything they truly needed was below the waves.

And then there was Calypso. Older than Amphitrite and the twins, but younger than some of the other nereids. Although she could be onerous, she wasn't always. Only when she was jealous or felt threatened in some way. It was clear she desired to occupy the thoughts and minds of everyone around her, and they had all come to accept her nature. Truth be told, Amphitrite found her more exhausting than anything.

Like any other family, her sisters possessed varying temperaments, with different combinations of traits inherited from their parents. They came by them honestly. While their father ruled with a surprisingly mild and gentle hand for a Titan, their mother, conversely, could be quite severe in both her mood and judgement. Thankfully for her children, the harshest of her brash and strong-willed nature had mellowed with age. A gentler side had emerged with each pregnancy, until she had settled into the role of nurturing mother.

That's not to say she didn't have her moments. As all goddesses must, Doris rarely showed weakness, keeping it well hidden behind a stunningly beautiful but oftentimes emotionless face.

Most of the nereids had been born kind-hearted and self-assured, but there were a few who had inherited less of these desirable qualities. Like Calypso, they were quite self-centered and spitefully jealous things, and would often target the meekest among them. Amphitrite was one of the nereids who avoided conflict. She preferred the company of sea creatures than most of her own sisters. For one thing, sea creatures were not envious of Amphitrite's hair, which was the color of a breathtaking golden dawn kissed by the ruby glow of a sunset, or that she danced so gracefully she would often garner praise from their critical mother.

That's not to say Nereus and Doris hadn't tried their best to dissuade pettiness among their daughters. But with so many, it wasn't always possible, which was why when Amphitrite was not dancing or swimming with Galene, she could be found miles away exploring some alcove or deep crag in the ocean floor, keeping company and taking care of her fellow sea creatures.

Suddenly, the clear blue water around her darkened to an icy gray, and the low rumble of moving earth reverberated in the distance. Amphitrite looked at the turtle with wide eyes, but it had tucked its head back into its shell. She stifled a panicked whimper. There was no time to be seized by her own fear. The creatures. She must make sure they were all tucked safely away before racing back to the castle.

She picked up the sea turtle and, reaching into the crevice all the way to her elbows, she placed it deep within the rock.

One by one, anemone closed in on themselves and the fish that had been floating peacefully only seconds before now frantically darted for safety. All the while the sea swayed, its stirring gaining speed and gathering strength until the long leafy strands of kelp growing around the reef whipped back and forth violently.

"Don't be frightened," she called out, reassuring the creatures. "His vexation will subside soon, and all will be calm. Be well, my friends."

Amphitrite pushed off the rock and turned toward home. The current was strong, and her arms quickly grew tired from straining. Against her better judgment she changed course, propelling herself upwards toward the surface. If she could catch a glimpse of the King, or what had raised his ire, perhaps she could help in some way.

She broke the surface, the waves churning and tossing her about as she treaded water. *This is folly. I should not be here.* She had never seen let alone been in the presence of the King of the Sea. What could she do?

Despite this, she swam closer to shore, dragging herself onto a slippery rock to survey her surroundings. As the wind lashed at her, she saw nothing but the stormy sea punishing the land around it.

Then, without warning, an enormous crack of lightning sounded from behind her. She hauled herself around just in time to witness jagged fingers of electricity grip the horizon. The darkened sky surged with a series of flashes, illuminating clouds so ominous it made her skin prickle.

Thinking better of her foolish notion to try and bring comfort to the tumultuous King of the Sea, Amphitrite dove back into the ocean and headed toward safety.

CHAPTER 2

Poseidon folded his arms, smiling triumphantly as he waited for King Cecrops to announce him as the winner. He had always been the patron deity of this *polis* by the sea. Despite Cecrops having seized it from another, Poseidon still protected all who sailed in and out of its port. It was the way of things. He watched over all who inhabited this land, which prospered in no small part because of the sea, and its people left offerings in his honor.

As ruler over the oceans, it was only natural this arrangement existed. He safeguarded these people, keeping them from harm's way, and they worshipped him in return. It was a simple exchange, an advantageous alliance, and a treaty in which he took great pride.

All had been right as rain, that is until Athena decided to challenge him for it. Now, here he stood, never having imagined he would be forced to compete for his people's favor.

He glanced at Athena, standing smug in both her armor and her audacity. She was the child of his brother Zeus, his favorite, in fact, who believed she was exempt from criticism or punishment, especially from her fellow Olympians.

Poseidon was Zeus's *brother*. If there was any one of them who should be untouchable, it was Poseidon. The King of the Gods had given rule over the sea to *him*, not Athena. She was the Goddess of War. What did she want with a city coated with salt and people who smelled of fish anyway?

Poseidon was convinced there was nothing more to it than her love of competition. Either she had been bored, or she had wanted a city of her own. How long had she been strategizing, thinking and rethinking her plan to selfishly snatch away something that was not hers?

No, it was no secret he and Athena did not get on well. He'd been content to avoid her for the most part, leaving her to meddle in others' affairs under the guise of *wisdom*, but when she had initiated this contest, well, Poseidon could not—would not—refuse.

Poseidon thrust his trident high into the air, unleashing a terrible roar as it came crashing back down to earth. How dare King Cecrops name Athena the victor. Did the man not have eyes? Could he not see how much stronger, how much more *passionate*, Poseidon was than his conceited, albeit cunning, gray-eyed niece?

A tidal wave formed when he dragged his three-pointed scepter along the bottom of the sea, sweeping away creatures large and small in its wake. What did he care? King Cecrops and his people should consider themselves lucky Poseidon had kept his composure for as long as he had. Fortunate for them, it had been long enough to get into his chariot and command his hippocampi to deliver him back to his golden palace.

In truth, he hadn't made it there. When he had gotten just far enough away from the newly named city of Athens, he had yanked the reins tight. The water horses had come to a halt, and he had gotten out of his chariot so he could unleash the rage inside of him.

He could have easily pummeled the man's city walls to crumbling bits. They all saw what had happened when he struck the rocky ground with is trident, had they not? How the river had sprung forth from the crack in the earth as a divine gift to them? Of course, it had filled with brackish water. What had they expected? He was King of the Sea, and what was his domain but salt and brine?

He slammed his fist down at the injustice, the sea racing toward the sky in a geyser of fury, clearing a path for it to hit the rocky bottom with a resounding boom. The ground shifted under his feet, as the small fissures gave way to wide cracks, swallowing the unfortunate beasts that had been left clinging to them.

If they had not known he was furious before, they certainly knew it now.

Both men and gods alike suffered his volatile nature, and although it was rare for anyone to witness one of his tantrums, they all felt it, both on land and in the sea.

His tempestuousness rivaled that of his notoriously hot-headed brother. Despite the ocean being Poseidon's domain, he would often make the ground tremble with his wrath, earning him the name Earth Shaker. It was a name he did not like. He could be calm and tranquil as well, and on the days when he was happy and content, the sea was calm.

Why did they only remember when his temper had gotten the best of him?

Amidst his display of indignance, Poseidon didn't notice how the white clouds gathered until they became dark and heavy. Nor did he hear the thunder rumble a warning from within as they billowed and rolled. It took a bolt of lightning to his trident for him to finally stop his ranting and raving.

Poseidon tensed, his jaw clenching as he absorbed the enormous shock of electricity. Icy regret flooded his veins at the same time the pain seized his muscles. The voltage snapped and crackled as it coursed through him, the intensity of it leaving him panting.

"You have my attention," said Poseidon through gritted teeth. His outburst had caught the attention of his brother, ruler over them all. Again. "Release me."

The pain moved from his limbs to his head when Poseidon heard his brother's voice in his mind. *Come to me and receive my counsel.*

Poseidon could do nothing but nod, and when he did, his suffering eased. It was sure to return, however. Zeus was not happy with him, that much was clear. Not that Poseidon fretted over this. He was one of the three strongest gods, sons of Chronus and Rhea, and feared nothing, not even his brother who'd saved him from the prison of his father's belly. The Titan had eaten his children out of fear when he'd heard a prophecy; they would be greater than him in both strength and name.

Although forever grateful to be rescued, Poseidon still found the irony humorous that

Zeus, after saving his brothers and sisters from a most terrible existence, went on to follow in the footsteps of their father, only this time devouring the mother instead of child.

The Fates had seen to it that Zeus understood the atrocity of consuming another, for no savior for this child had been required. Zeus's head had violently split wide open to release Athena, the cunning goddess of wisdom who had been born fully formed.

Athena, the bane of his existence who could do no wrong in his brother's eyes, even though she had caused him much pain. The spiteful goddess who had outwitted him to a city now called Athens in her honor.

Poseidon's nostrils flared at the injustice. How easily things came to her, and to all the others, while he had to fight for every bit of fame he got. He was as powerful as Zeus, as cunning as Hades. Poseidon could make the earth *move*.

Sometimes he felt like Ares, the God of War; tormented from constantly battling foes both seen and unseen. Except, he could destroy the seen, he had proven that during the war against the Titans. It was the unseen, the battles that lived in his head and in his heart, he could not seem to conquer. It was why he had decided long ago that if no one could see the good in him, he would make sure they saw the bad.

With a huff of irritation, he launched himself into the sky, his sights set on Olympus.

CHAPTER 3

Poseidon had returned to his own throne room, where he sat brooding and sipping wine. The golden goblet in his hand matched the golden throne where he sat, which gleamed like the many gilded frames hung on the walls around him. In fact, his whole palace was made of pure gold, shining under the waves like a wishing well full of polished coins.

He lifted the cup to his lips once more, only this time he swallowed the rest of the sweet liquid in one great gulp. The summons to Olympus had been just as he had expected; Zeus repeating the same reprimands as he had countless times before, in the same stern tone.

"Your violent outbursts are no good for any of us, brother." Zeus had stated the obvious calmly, but Poseidon had seen the way the tiny arcs of electricity had jumped between his brother's fingers, ready to form into bolts of lightning at the slightest provocation.

"It is the way of things," Poseidon had responded, truly dismayed his own brother was wary of him enough to keep his defenses at the ready. "I like it no more than you. It's..." The bitter truth of his dual nature—incredibly beautiful to behold, horribly ugly to bear—had resigned him. "A most terrible thing. What would you have me do?"

Their brother Hades, who was no less powerful but not so quick to anger as Poseidon and Zeus, could not understand the violent outbursts that plagued them, Poseidon more so than Zeus. It seemed Poseidon had inherited all the ill-tempered parts of their father, while Hades and Zeus possessed the better qualities, like cunning and will power. Qualities that made others fall in line with a look or a word.

No one listened to Poseidon unless he used force.

At least Zeus could sympathize with him. Poseidon knew this to be true simply by the number of times he'd been in the same position, having the same conversation. He was grateful for Zeus's benevolence toward him, but Poseidon still bristled at his brother's tenacity.

Poseidon supposed both of those qualities, along with his mighty physical strength and equally magnanimous disposition, was why Zeus was the King of the Gods, and not him or Hades.

"Marry," Zeus had said, as if it would simplify things instead of complicating them.

"Marry?" Poseidon hadn't been sure whether to laugh or scoff at the idea. He was of the mind that a marriage would most definitely not curb his outbursts but make them worse. So, Poseidon had promptly refused to entertain his brother's suggestion. "No."

He had enjoyed the company of women plenty but had never considered marrying any of them, mostly because he hadn't encountered one he thought could tolerate his moods, let alone his temper. Truth be told, finding someone who could handle him not only seemed like a long and laborious task, but a huge undertaking he wasn't sure he had the patience to see through.

But Hades had found Persephone, hadn't he?

The Fates had brought Hades and Persephone together, true enough, but the sisters despised Poseidon. Why else would they weave the threads of his life to include such a contentious nature?

Zeus had sighed, more loudly than Poseidon had ever heard him do so before. "I grow tired of this conversation, brother. The choice is yours, but I implore you, please consider it. The sooner you find happiness, the better. If not for yourself, then for the rest of us..."

A high-pitched clicking scattered Poseidon's thoughts, bringing him back into the present.

"Shall I call for more wine, my Lord?" said Delphin, an old sea daemon in his service.

Delphin wasn't so much as a servant as a trusted companion. He appeared as though he were half man, half dolphin, and had arrived at the palace long ago, to pay respect to the newly crowned King of the Sea.

The daemon had an easy way about him. Although he was somewhat of an opportunist, he was generous and kind, blessed with a quick wit and a silver tongue. Poseidon had no doubt Delphin could sell bread to a baker should he find himself in need of it.

From the moment Delphin had arrived at court, he'd known what to do or say to keep Poseidon in good cheer. They had gotten on so well, in fact, the daemon had simply never left.

"Only if you join me in drowning my sorrows," said Poseidon.

"That can certainly be arranged," replied Delphin.

He lifted a hand, clicking and whistling until a cupbearer scuttled into the room. The crablike creature clutched a goblet in each of its spotted claws. It scurried over to Poseidon and Delphin, both having to reach down to take the cups from it. After bowing, it left them to their conversation.

Delphin took a sip. "Even watered down, the wine here is still the finest in all the sea—"

"Zeus commands me to marry," said Poseidon, not waiting for Delphin to finish.

Delphin's round black eyes went wide, making them appear larger and even more wideset than they already were. "He commands it?"

"Not outright," clarified Poseidon, "But he strongly suggests it, which is one and the same." Poseidon chuckled to himself. "He is being careful. He knows the trouble that would follow if he *commanded* me to do anything."

"I see," said Delphin, reading between the lines. "Well, then we must find you a wife!"

"And how do you propose *we* do that?" replied Poseidon. "No Olympian goddess will have me, Hecate and her witches despise me, and there are no uncoupled Titans left, not that I'm aware of, anyway."

"Ah, my Lord, this may be true, but there are plenty of beautiful fish in your seas," said Delphin. "Why, the Titan, Nereus, whose fiefdom is not far from here, has fifty daughters alone. He is descended from friends of the Olympians, not foes, am I right? Surely there would be one among them who would be honored to be your queen."

Poseidon knew of Nereus's daughters, renowned for their dancing. Being nymphs, he imagined they were known for other things as well. Why hadn't he considered it before?

"I'm listening," he said, arching a brow. The thought did pique his interest. Although it may be a marriage of convenience, a well-disposed nymph could make the perfect consort.

"I'm certain Nereus would agree to strengthening the alliance between his family and yours," said Delphin.

"Yes, I'm sure he will. The question is, would Doris?" said Poseidon. He had always found the sea god amenable; it was his headstrong wife who might not agree to marry off one of their daughters to an Olympian. "She is the one who truly rules there."

"There is only one way to find out," replied Delphin, his dolphin's smile growing wider, showing his long rows of teeth.

"What terms would you bring to her on my behalf?"

"That she be granted a full moon to prepare. During that time, the nereids will practice a special dance for you. At the end of it, Nereus will hold a feast in your honor, where you will choose the daughter who catches your eye."

Poseidon stroked his short-cropped beard, thinking about the proposal. Patience wasn't his strong suit, but he could try, especially if it meant Zeus would no longer pester him about taking a wife. Besides, he did so enjoy pomp and circumstance.

"Very well," said Poseidon, liking the idea more and more. "Go to Nereus and Doris with those terms."

Delphin bobbed his long, bottled nose before diving backward and twisting, his flippered feet propelling him toward an ornate archway.

"Delphin?" Poseidon called out to the daemon, just before he slipped out the door.

Delphin looped around. "Yes, my Lord?"

What would he do without this silver-tongued sea daemon on his side? The only friend he had in all the oceans. Hopefully, he would soon have more. And a wife.

"As always, your counsel has been good, old friend," said Poseidon. "I think this idea of yours just might work."

CHAPTER 4

Amphitrite waited patiently for her turn to enter the throng of swirling-haired sea nymphs. For the past few weeks, their mother had been gathering them early each morning to dance.

It was well known, among the gods as well as in the mortal world, nymphs loved to revel. River, tree, mountain, even the more serious meadow, it was no secret their kind took great pleasure in the wild abandon dancing provided. Nereids were no exception. As far as she was concerned, twirling and laughing among her sisters was the best way to start the day.

Her mother, a lovely dancer herself, nodded at the carefully orchestrated formation before them. "Now, Amphitrite."

Upon her mother's urging, Amphitrite swam into alignment next to Galene and began performing a series of graceful movements they had been taught. Their dance was usually not so intricate, but they were to have a guest in a few weeks' time, and mother had decided the special dance they were to perform needed to be more synchronized 'so that each girl had an equal chance,' as she had put it.

An equal chance at what? The comment had given Amphitrite pause when her mother had said it, but her sisters, including Galene, had begun to whisper excitedly among themselves.

Unlike the others, Amphitrite had frowned, having no idea why they acted with such giddiness. She suspected it had to do with what the older girls talked about so often—men, marriage, and children—and had promptly dismissed it.

She was never getting married.

"Absolutely beautiful, Amphitrite," her mother called out. "You move even more gracefully than the waves."

Amphitrite beamed at the compliment, elated at her mother's approval. It didn't come often. Her smile dropped, however, when she spied Calypso glaring at her as she swam toward her.

Calypso swept one arm upward in a grand arc. "Perhaps. But is she charming enough to catch the eye of a king?" she said before twirling away.

The comment did more than confuse Amphitrite, it stung. Calypso's words had been mean-spirited and wounding. Her sister had a habit of projecting her insecurities on others, and it saddened Amphitrite Calypso could not see herself the way others did. She was as beautiful as any nymph, perhaps more so, with her driftwood hair and striking teal eyes. True, she could work on being more kind, but she was outgoing and charismatic, achieving whatever she set her mind to. Calypso would make a wonderful consort to whatever sea god came looking for a wife.

Amphitrite's stomach looped at the thought. Would she herself make a good match? She thought she would, but she could scarcely imagine leaving this part of the sea to do so. She was perfectly content caring for those around her, including her parents. In fact, she had decided long ago she would remain in her father's palace forever.

"All right, that's enough for now," said Doris, clapping to get everyone's attention. "You are dismissed for the day. I dare say most of you are ready."

The group dispersed, with Galatea immediately heading in the direction of the shore. Galene, however, made a beeline for Amphitrite with a heart-warming smile. It was so bright Amphitrite had no choice but to beam back. Maybe Galene would go exploring with her this afternoon.

When she was close enough, Galene linked an arm with Amphitrite, pulling her towards one of the many spacious common rooms of the castle reserved for frolicking or playing games in between mealtimes.

"Did you hear what mother said? We are ready!" cried Galene excitedly. A moment later her shoulders dropped, her brow furrowing. "Or some of us are, anyway."

Galene was not the best dancer.

"You'll do fine, Galene," said Amphitrite. "It's not as though our guest will be King Poseidon himself."

Her laughter was cut short when Galene halted suddenly, Amphitrite having no choice but to stop as well.

"Amphitrite," said Galene, unlocking arms and turning to face her. "It *is* King Poseidon who comes. He is to choose a queen."

Amphitrite's mouth dropped open, trying to remember when her mother had said this. She scoured her memory, and although she recalled they were to dance at an upcoming feast, she could not call to mind exactly who their mother said they would be entertaining.

Poseidon? How in the world had she missed *that*? Had she been far away, at the reef petting turtles, or swimming with whales? She must have been.

"I... I..." stammered Amphitrite. "I didn't know."

Galene shot her an incredulous look, both eyebrows sliding up. "Truly?"

Amphitrite tugged on the ends of her hair, as she often did when agitated. "I knew mother and father were to host a feast for a guest of honor, and we were to dance, but I assumed it might be Phorcys... or Pontus, perhaps... or..."

Her algae-green eyes flashing with warning, Galene shook her head slightly, signaling for Amphitrite to stop speaking. She clamped her mouth shut when the water behind her swayed with movement, but it was too late.

"What's the matter, Amphitrite?" said Calypso, inserting herself into the conversation. "Worried you're not good enough?"

Proud of herself, Calypso laughed loudly.

"Hush!" said Galene. "Amphitrite is the best dancer of us all. I think it is *you* who is worried."

Calypso planted her hands on her hips. "Is that so? Well, *I'm* a good dancer," she said, placing a finger on her chest. "And if Amphitrite is the best, as you say, then it must be *you* who is worried?"

Galene looked as though she might cry, obviously goaded by their older sister's taunt. Why did Calypso have to be so relentless? They were family. If they couldn't love one another, couldn't they at least be civil?

Amphitrite narrowed her eyes at Calypso. "Enough," she said. "We are *all* good dancers." She took Galene's hand and began to lead her away.

"Perhaps," replied Calypso, determined to get the last word. "But who among us is bold enough to be a queen?"

CHAPTER 5

Poseidon looked on as Delphin pulled on the reins, slowing a pair of giant horses to a stop in front of a castle made of mottled rock. It was built into the side of an underwater cliff, and although it didn't gleam like his massive palace, it was still large enough to be impressive.

When the chariot finally came to a stop, Poseidon nodded at the Titan ruler and his consort, who were standing outside to greet him. It seemed this potential alliance was off to a good start.

He surveyed the line of nereids standing behind Nereus and Doris, gripping his trident so tightly his knuckles ached. There were indeed fifty of them, and they were all looking directly at him.

All except one. Her golden ruby-kissed hair floated around her prettily as she gazed at his sea horses, her lips quirked in a smile. She looked at them as though she wanted to wrap her arms around their wild necks. They were magnificent creatures, if he did say so himself. Her appreciation amused him enough to loosen his fingers and cradle the heavy scepter instead of choke it.

"I present your majesty and supreme ruler, King Poseidon," announced Delphin, rolling a hand toward the sandy ocean floor as he bowed in Poseidon's direction.

He hadn't even noticed Delphin exit the chariot, but now that his arrival had been announced there was no turning back. After this evening, he would have a queen. It was exhilarating and terrifying all at once, and it made his heart pound and stomach churn.

Nereus bowed, his unbound white hair rippling behind him. Doris's hair was the color of kelp, complementing the pinks and golds of her tall crown of shells. She and her daughters curtsied, and Poseidon couldn't stop himself from glancing at the nymph with the sunset in her hair. He half expected her to still be preoccupied with the horses, but her eyes were now downcast like the rest of them.

Normally, Poseidon enjoyed these displays of devotion, lived for it, but for some reason he could not explain, he suddenly felt uneasy. A thought formed in the back of his mind. He wasn't always benevolent. It was no secret, least of all to him, he was bad-tempered and prone to ill-behavior. Such was the way of gods, but it did make him wonder if they knelt out of loyalty or fear.

"Welcome, welcome!" replied Nereus, opening his arms wide. "We are honored to host the King of the Sea." He gestured toward the grand double doors of his castle. "Come, let us go inside and celebrate your long-awaited and most anticipated arrival."

The line of nereids parted to either side, allowing room for Nereus and Poseidon to head into the castle first. Delphin, ever the charming gentleman, offered his elbow to Doris, who accepted, and they followed closely behind.

"My wife and I are thrilled for this alliance," said Nereus as they walked. "As you can imagine, our daughters are delighted as well." He gave a slight chuckle. "It's all they have been talking about since the sea daemon came with your proposal."

"I am pleased by the warm welcome, Nereus," replied Poseidon. "And I look forward to making the acquaintance of your daughters."

One in particular, as it was turning out.

They passed through an intricately carved triple arch and into a columnated foyer where the tiled floor shimmered with iridescent abalone shells. Further inside the castle, Nereus led Poseidon up a grand staircase to a sitting room where, he was informed, they could recline and relax while the noonday meal was prepared.

When they were ready, they would head into the back courtyard, where they would lunch in Doris's prized kelp garden. Afterward, he would be shown to private quarters so that he and his companion could refresh themselves before moving to the dining hall, where they would eat the finest food and witness the loveliest dancing in all the seven seas.

Although Poseidon had enjoyed the hospitality throughout the day, he unleashed a heavy sigh of relief when he and Delphin were finally shown to a spacious and finely appointed private room in one of several castle towers.

"Well, what a splendid way to spend the day, don't you agree?" said Delphin, pouring wine into a conch shell. Poseidon nodded at him to pour a second. "I daresay my suggestion was fate, my Lord. So many beautiful women to choose from. I can hardly wait for this evening's performance. You must be positively desperate for the night to begin."

Poseidon took the proffered wine before drinking deep. Should he ask Delphin if he knew the name of the rose gold nymph? He couldn't seem to stop thinking about her.

"My Lord?"

Poseidon shook his head, pulling his thoughts back into the present and out of the future.

"I'm sorry, old friend," he replied, still swaying from the involuntary ripple he'd sent throughout the ocean with his overthinking. "This is much more overwhelming than I thought it would be. These women, they seem so eager to marry a stranger, one they do not fully know."

"My Lord," said Delphin. "Why do you speak lowly of yourself?"

"You and I both know I have a terrible temper," replied Poseidon. "I cannot hold it in check for long. I have tried, Delphin, but I have failed, many times. What woman would want to be avowed to a tyrant?" He tipped his cup and finished the wine Delphin had poured for him. "Perhaps this was a mistake."

Delphin paced back and forth, and Poseidon knew what was coming next. Delphin had not been moved by Poseidon's lament, and the old sea daemon was not willing to let him give up so easily.

"Every king has a way about him that makes him great, or else he would not be so," began Delphin. "Zeus wears the armor of audacity, Hades a shroud of mystery. And you..." He made the imploring gestures of a scholar to emphasize the elegant words of a poet. "You, my Lord, possess the spark of passion. What good is greatness without a fire to light the way? You have felt the evidence of it mere minutes ago. Only a ripple, was it not?" Delphin lifted an eyebrow. "No tidal wave at your upset. No quaking earth at your unease. I believe there is one woman who balances you, simply by being near her, and as fate would have it, she is here, in this very castle."

Delphin gave Poseidon a knowing look before taking a sip of wine, but he wasn't convinced the Fates would do anything of the sort. Not for him, anyway.

"I don't know if I believe all that, Delphin," murmured Poseidon. "Alas, even if it turns out to be true, I fear this would only be a marriage of convenience."

"What marriage isn't, my Lord? If your queen does not grow to love you, she will learn to accept you. Besides, you know Zeus will not relent until you do what he wants. If he thinks marriage is the answer..." Delphin shrugged.

"We are already here. Promise an old friend you'll keep an open mind."

Poseidon nodded, reassured enough by the daemon to at least do that. But even though his heart hoped for a blissful marriage, his mind insisted it was improbable, perhaps even impossible.

CHAPTER 6

Amphitrite followed along with the rest of the nereids as her father led King Poseidon into the castle. She bit the inside of her cheek to keep from joining in the whispers about how impossibly tall he was, and the luxurious way his sandy hair flowed over his shoulders and down his muscled back.

Instead, she kept her assessment of him to herself. Of course, they had all noticed the shade of his smooth skin, browned by the sun, but had they noticed his eyes? Had they, too, been taken aback at how brightly they shined, like two pieces of polished jade? She had imagined them to be the hues of the ocean—a cold stormy gray—but they were as warm as the blue-green waters of the Aegean coast.

He was neither young nor old, but in his prime, effortlessly embodying both the earth and the sea. She thought the hair covering his strong jaw would have been as light as the waves upon his head, but it was slightly darker and tinged with red, proving that such contrasts could be utterly captivating. He truly was divine to behold, and the thought of him coming here, to her father's domain to find a wife, made Amphitrite's heart flutter in her chest against its will.

She had never met an Olympian god or goddess before, let alone one so beguiling. So great was her awe, she found it easier to focus her attention on the glorious white horses harnessed to his golden chariot. It was the only way she could keep herself from staring at him as wide-eyed and agape as a child.

What did you expect? He's an Olympian, one of the three most powerful besides.

Once they were through the courtyard and inside the keep, Nereus turned and dismissed them, bidding them farewell until that evening. Amphitrite and Galene smiled prettily, curtseying politely with the rest of the nereids before proceeding to their favorite room inside the castle.

It was a comfortable space to convalesce, with soft sea moss to lay and stone benches to sit while gazing at the grand murals. There hadn't been a time Amphitrite had entered it and not admired the expansive panoramas gracing the walls. They bore the images of her father's Titan brethren, telling the origin stories that utterly fascinated her.

She especially liked the wall dedicated to Oceanus and Tethys, the Titans who had been so in love they'd populated the world with countless oceanids. In fact, they were so smitten with one another, they were too preoccupied to fight against Zeus in the Titanomachy. As a reward, Zeus thanked them by allowing them to continue to reign over their watery kingdoms unbothered.

"Isn't this all so exciting?" said Galene, scattering Amphitrite's thoughts. "Come, I'll plait your hair, and then you can help me with mine."

Amphitrite nodded, allowing Galene to pull her over to a reclining sofa nestled into one of the many alcoves throughout the room. Once settled, Galene gently combed her fingers through Amphitrite's hair. The repetitive motion relaxed her, and her mind began to wander again.

She had never understood the lure of marriage, but she did know the power of love. The evidence of it was right there before her, painted on the walls in vibrant color. She tried to keep her mind from picturing what it would be like to be married to an Olympian god, so in love and full of contentment their only concern was each other and the family they'd created.

But keeping the thought out of her mind was impossible. King Poseidon was no longer a figment of her imagination, an unseen god wreaking havoc from a distance. No, he was *here*, in all his glory and magnificent flesh, and he had come to choose a wife. One who could settle him, she suspected, for she had seen past the exquisite cold, hard exterior and ventured into the warm depths of his eyes.

Her desire for him bloomed low in her belly, until the core of her went soft and slick as a jellyfish. She gasped when she realized *this* was what made her sisters giggle so girlishly, even the oldest of them, and flush so thoroughly.

"Have I pulled too tight?" asked Galene.

"No," replied Amphitrite, wrapping her arms around her ribs to keep herself from squirming out of her skin. "I'm just a little nervous is all."

"Hold still, then, sister," said Galene. "You do want to look your best for King Poseidon, don't you?"

It was a harmless question, but it made Amphitrite's stomach loop. She'd seen the narrow-eyed gazes directed at her whenever their mother raved about her dancing. Her poise, her grace, her hair. These were the things they held against her—not Galene or Galatea, of course, but the older nereids, and a handful of the younger ones—even though these gifts that had been bestowed upon her were out of her control.

She did not want to give them more to be envious about.

"It seems the jitters have gotten the best of me," Amphitrite reached up and stilled Galene's hand. She would dim her light, so the others, including Galene, could shine brighter. "Perhaps we do your hair first."

CHAPTER 7

Garlands of seaweed were lavishly draped and pinned to the dining hall tables. Glints of silver lit the space like fireflies as tiny fish darted in between the long line of fluted columns. The underbelly of a large school of tuna flashed, before turning suddenly and heading in the opposite direction from which it came. When the room darkened and he looked up to see an enormous whale pass overhead, Poseidon couldn't help but be impressed.

A band of musicians played lyres made of tortoise shells while the servants laid platters and bowls of delicacies before him. Instead of reaching for a plate, he took up a wine glass. He couldn't possibly eat his fill when his stomach twisted so tightly.

He inhaled deeply, fortifying his careful façade of calm. What did he have to be so riled about? He was *the* god of the sea. Any woman would be honored to be his queen. Likewise, as Delphin had said, she would eventually grow to love him.

Or had he said she would learn to accept him? Either way, whoever she turned out to be, he felt as though he had already let her down.

The music swelled to a stop before playing anew. It was an upbeat march, to signify the start of the dance. A round of awed gasps and polite clapping intermingled with the music as the curtains framing the stage slid open, revealing the nereids already in their positions.

They were all beautiful, adorned with glittering starfish, lustrous strands of pearls, and colorful seagrass. Some were clad in octopi, using the long tentacles as flowing skirts, while others had no need, for their fish tails were covered in shimmering rainbow scales and diaphanous fins.

Poseidon's gaze searched for the nymph who'd caught his attention earlier. He bit the inside of his cheek to keep from grinning when he found her. She stood near the back of the formation, staring ahead motionless. Her arms were raised, and one leg extended behind her as she waited for the dance to begin.

She wore no brightly hued anemone or iridescent mother of pearl, but only a diadem of barnacles. They were ugly parasitic creatures that were pale and lusterless, but somehow, when encircled upon her head, made the golden-haired beauty more stunning than the rest.

It would do no good to give away his interest before the dancing had even begun, so he forced his gaze to continue over the rest of the nymphs. It stopped, doubling back when he spied a nereid with silt-colored hair tinged with the barest reflection of a blue sky. She was staring directly at him with a gaze that was as intense as her striking teal eyes.

Poseidon didn't break eye contact with her, and, to his surprise, she did not look away. Her cheeks slowly pushed into a bashful smile.

Or was it a triumphant grin?

"Her name is Calypso, Your Majesty," said Nereus, seated to Poseidon's right. "And she is as bold as she is beautiful."

Poseidon was not surprised by Nereus's attentiveness. Being in such an honored position as father of the bride, of course Nereus would be watching Poseidon carefully. It was in his best interest to give counsel on which of his daughters might make the best match for a long and prosperous alliance.

"Who is she?" asked Poseidon, nodding at the nymph with the barnacle diadem.

"That is Amphitrite," said Doris, leaning slightly into his left side. "Reserved but one of our most gifted dancers. Perhaps even our best."

Poseidon swallowed hard. Amphitrite. What a lovely name.

"If you are looking for a strong-willed queen, you might also consider Thetis," said Nereus.

"What about Galatea?" said Doris through pursed lips. "There, the one with the alabaster skin, dressed in shells."

"Lovely," replied Poseidon.

And it was true, they were all pleasing to look upon. He could see why Doris suggested Galatea, but he could feel there was something more to it than her dreamy-eyed beauty. He was sure they all had one quality or another that would make them suitable for the role, but the suggestion felt as though it had been made for Galatea's benefit and not his.

It did not matter, however, because his thoughts hadn't strayed far from Amphitrite. Nor had his gaze, it seemed, not until it was suddenly forced to cut to Calypso, who had left the formation and was now approaching the dais.

"Calypso?" said Doris sternly to the nymph standing before her. "What is the meaning of this? The dance is about to begin."

Calypso curtsied before speaking. "I'm sorry, mother, but there has been a question that has been plaguing my mind all morning." She shot a quick glance at Poseidon, her tongue darting over her lips. "I'm afraid I won't be able to do my best if I do not know the answer, and I do so want to do my best."

Nereus sighed heavily. "Calypso, this is most disrupt—"

Poseidon lifted a hand.

"It's all right, Nereus," he said. "What is your question?"

Calypso's gaze shifted down to her dainty bejeweled feet while clearing her throat demurely. Poseidon's brow itched to furrow—where had her confidence suddenly gone—but he willed his expression to remain passive.

"Will his Majesty be spending time with us individually," she said, peeking up at him through long lashes. "In order to base his choice on more than appearance and dancing alone?"

Poseidon tilted his head. This one had moxie, to be sure. However, he had a strange feeling there was something sinister lying just below the surface. Based on his earlier interaction with her, and how intensely she had looked at him, this display of simpering seemed like more of an act, a devious attempt to pull his attention away from the others and place it directly on herself.

She'd succeeded, he would give her that. Whether she would be able to hold his attention and for how long, he could not say.

"It is a fair question," he replied. "Calypso, is it?"

"Yes, King Poseidon," she replied with a sly smile. "I am Calypso."

"But, your Majesty, there are fifty of them!" cried Nereus. "It would take days to get to know them all, and the wedding has been agreed upon for tomorrow morning."

Poseidon resisted the urge to clench his jaw. He had a reputation for being quick tempered. He did not want to add rash and unjust to the list. This nymph had cunningly backed him into a corner.

But he knew the game she played—he'd fallen prey to it many times with Athena—and he countered her move accordingly.

"Since you care so greatly for your sisters, and that all of you get an equal chance at being chosen," he said, taking care the words did not pass through pursed lips. He knew that was not the case at all, and he could not resist letting her know he would not be trifled with. "I shall

take it upon myself to dance with four of you, so
that I may be sure to choose the right sister.”

CHAPTER 8

Amphitrite's limbs shook from holding their position for so long. She could see Nereus and Doris, looking on with interest, but the back of Calypso's head obscured the King's face. What was Calypso doing? Amphitrite could hardly believe her sister had been brazened enough to address him; about what she could only guess.

Perhaps Galatea was missing? Amphitrite scanned the row ahead and to her left, to where Galatea stood staring off into the distance dreamily, just like always. Her gaze darted around the group. Dero, Erato, Neso; all there. Amphitrite pondered what could be important enough to delay the dance when Calypso turned around and made her way back to the group. Amphitrite searched her sister's face for any sign of trouble, but the only thing she found was a satisfied smirk.

Before she could think on it more, the music began, and the nereids started to move. Amphitrite knew the dance well, and while she sashayed across the stage, jumping and twirling effortlessly, Galene struggled to keep up, no doubt her nerves getting the best of her.

Amphitrite tried not to grimace when Galene quickly fell behind, her face flushing a deeper crimson with every missed step.

Calypso spun by in a series of pirouettes just then, sniggering as she passed. Amphitrite struggled to keep the smile on her face, but it was a difficult task. Judging by their delighted expressions, it was clear the court didn't suspect a thing, but Amphitrite knew. Calypso's devious smile had been proof. She had deployed one of her schemes again, to get attention, and it made Amphitrite angry.

Galene's distressed breathing and panicked whimpers scattered Amphitrite's thoughts, but only temporarily.

Calypso knows Galene rattles easily. She also knows I would sacrifice my performance to calm her. Careful to keep a cheerful demeanor, Amphitrite broke formation and danced over to Galene.

"Pretend it is just us," she whispered, taking her sister's hands and swinging her around in a circle. "Focus on me, Galene, and you will find the music again."

Amphitrite let go of her sister's hands, but kept her eyes locked on Galene as she led her through a series of moves. She nodded encouragingly, repeating the movements with her until they were finally in sync with one another.

"Yes, that's it, Galene," said Amphitrite. "There is no one else here. Just you and me, dancing on the shore under the moonlight."

Galene nodded, a tentative smile returning to her face. Amphitrite continued to go through the rudimentary series of movements, and with each sweep of their arms and sway of their hips, Galene gained more confidence.

"Excellent," whispered Amphitrite, remaining by Galene's side to perform the less impressive parts of the routine their mother had taught them.

She continued this way until Galene had fully regained her composure. After a slight nod from her, Amphitrite returned to her place among the more advanced group.

For the rest of the dance, Amphitrite kept a close watch on Calypso, to make sure she kept her distance from Galene. There would be no chance of recovery should Calypso manage to aim another round of insults at her.

Amphitrite breathed a sigh of relief when the end of the dance neared. This would be over soon. King Poseidon would choose Calypso, they would be wed, and when they left for his golden palace, the rest of them could get back to their lives. She suspected most of her sisters would lament at not being chosen, but they would eventually get over it.

As if he knew she was thinking about him, she felt the weight of the King's stare on her. He'd been stealing glances at her from the moment he'd arrived. Amphitrite thought it had been her imagination, but every time she dared to meet his eyes, sure enough, they had been fixed on her. They would, of course, immediately dart away like minnows. Imagine that. The King of the Sea, too nervous to hold the gaze of a nymph.

Her cheeks warmed as she thought about what the stolen glances might mean. Did she feel embarrassment or delight? It was a little of both, she supposed. As much as she wished it weren't so, the thought of being chosen as King Poseidon's bride, she must admit, did excite her, even despite her conviction to remain unwed.

The end of the dance came, and one by one, they began to form a long tunnel. Each nereid was to pass through it before bowing or curtsying to the King. One last chance to get noticed.

Amphitrite saw that Calypso was on the end, the most prime position to leave a lasting impression. A calculated move by Calypso to be the last nymph King Poseidon saw before making his decision. An image of Calypso antagonizing him, as was her nature, causing his moods to be even more tumultuous flashed in Amphitrite's mind. Without thinking, she took a place across from Calypso, who shot her a thin-lipped smile.

"Calypso," whispered Amphitrite. When her sister did not respond, she spoke louder. "Calypso." And louder still. "Calypso!"

When Calypso finally addressed her, she said, "Be quiet and leave me be."

"Have you no shame at all?" replied Amphitrite, undeterred.

"I have no idea what you mean."

"He will choose you," insisted Amphitrite, ignoring Calypso's feigned ignorance. "There is no need to be cruel."

Calypso huffed, dropping her act. "Will he? None of us can compete with you based on beauty and dance prowess alone, so I have taken matters into my own hands, and if using Galene as a means to an end is what needs to be done, then so be it."

"A means to an end?"

"Don't be so daft, Amphitrite," spat Calypso. "Isn't it obvious? Anyone who has eyes can see how he looks at you. You're beautiful *and* the best dancer. I stand no chance against you if the King is to base his decision on those two things alone. How can he see how brilliant my mind is when he is blinded by your beauty? I want out of this place, Amphitrite, so I took it upon myself to convince him to choose more than one of us, at least initially."

Amphitrite stood there, stunned. Shock and anger pulsed in her veins, leaving her hot and cold at once. It coursed through her, leaving her grappling. Calypso cared so little for her sisters and the life they lived she intended to use marriage as an escape. She did not want a loving union, she wanted a way out, and Amphitrite could scarcely believe her own flesh and blood had been born so ruthless.

"I refuse to apologize for making my own luck," snarled Calypso. "I swear to the gods, Amphitrite, if you ruin this for me, I will never forgive you."

Then, rubbing more salt in the wound, she turned toward King Poseidon, flashed him a most winning smile, and curtsied as though she had already gone from nymph to queen.

CHAPTER 9

Poseidon clapped politely at the impressive acrobatics some of the women performed. The dancing had just begun, but he wondered how much longer it would go on. He'd already made his choice and didn't care to see more, but, thanks to one meddling nereid, he was forced to prolong the process.

He released a soundless sigh, irritated but supposing it was ultimately a good thing. In this case, it probably wasn't prudent to go on outward appearances alone. If a marriage was to be rushed, the least he could do was make sure it lasted. The woman he chose needed to be, at the very least, companionable.

Although he tried not to be obvious, his gaze found Amphitrite wherever she was on the dancefloor. Doris was right. She was the best dancer, moving with such elegance and grace it captivated him. His heart leapt in his chest as he watched her, hoping the pounding could only be heard by his ears.

It wasn't the first time his pulse raced like this, no, but it was usually from anger, or a close match between competitors, not a woman dancing. Suddenly, he was irritated he'd been tricked. Prolonging this would only waste time, would it not? What point was there in choosing four of them instead of the one he truly desired?

He had given his word, that was the point. Not only to Nereus and Doris, but he'd also promised Delphin he would keep an open mind. He was an Olympian, and although he may be easily offended, with a penchant toward cold hard revenge when he had been, he always kept his word.

The nereids continued to swirl on stage until Poseidon thought he might expire. He was on the verge of begging Doris to cut the dance short when Amphitrite suddenly rushed over to help a nereid who seemed to be tripping over her own two feet.

Something gripped him at the sight of this, and the image of her ocean eyes locked on his, her fingertips smoothing his furrowed brow as she spoke to him gently, flashed in his mind. He closed his eyes, to try and hold on to the image. Was it possible that Delphin was right? The Fates had indeed put someone on this bedraggled earth to be his other half?

If he thought he was captivated before, now he was enraptured, and much closer to believing in destiny. *If she is truly the one,* he silently prayed to The Fates, the only deities more powerful than he, *let her feel the same.*

Poseidon opened his eyes to discover the nereids had made a tunnel. He nodded at each one benevolently when it was their time to bow or curtsy, even Thetis, who scowled at him petulantly. Calypso came second to last, beaming at him maniacally.

The music climbed to a crescendo before ending on a series of trilling high notes. *Thank the Fates* thought Poseidon, smiling wide and clapping loudly.

The only nereid left was Amphitrite, shoulders slumped, eyes downcast. He held his breath. Why did she look so vexed? He stared at her intently, willing her to lift her gaze, so she could look into his eyes and see how invested in her he already was. He felt his heart pound in his chest, heard it in his ears.

She did not look at him, only stared ahead blankly before bowing her head.

"Wonderful! Wonderful!" called out Nereus, applauding his nereids with pride. "Thank you, daughters." He motioned toward the empty tables reserved for them. "Please, have a seat and enjoy a bit of food and drink while King Poseidon makes his choice."

They dispersed, Amphitrite one of the last to make her way toward the long tables. Calypso had been the first, already securing a seat closest to the dais, with the clearest line of vision to the royal table.

"Nereus," said Doris coolly. "You forgot to announce King Poseidon will be dancing with four of them individually." She turned toward Poseidon. "Have you made your choice?"

"I have," he replied, stroking his bearded jaw. "I will dance with the four you have suggested, Galatea, Thetis, Calypso, and... Amphitrite."

"Very good," she nodded before leaning forward in anticipation. "Go ahead with the announcement, Nereus."

Nereus stood and cleared his throat. "Ladies and gentlemen of the court, your attention, please."

Just then, Poseidon realized he had not addressed the court or the nereids directly this entire time. He'd been content to let Nereus speak for him, and wondered if this made him look weak.

"Allow me," said Poseidon, standing and silencing Nereus by placing a hand on his shoulder. The old Titan nodded, conceding to the request and taking his seat once more.

The murmuring had been loud, and so Poseidon raised his voice. "Nereids!"

They flinched in unison, gasping in surprise. Or was it fear? He hadn't intended to intimidate them, but there was no going back and so he forged ahead.

"What the bards say is true," he continued. "There is not another creature alive that dances so gracefully and lovely as a nymph. Well done, ladies. I am most pleased with your beauty and talent. So much so, that four of you have caught my eye." He hoped they could not detect his lie. "I shall choose four of you to dance with, one song each, so that I may learn the truth of your heart."

A mix of shock and delight rippled through the crowd. Poseidon waited until the murmurs settled. He wanted the court's full attention when he spoke.

"The four I choose are Thetis, Galatea, Calypso, and Amphitrite."

The court burst into applause, and he forced his gaze toward the stage, so that he would not look at Amphitrite. Was she delighted or dismayed at his announcement?

I will find out soon enough.

He made his way toward the stairs leading up to the platform, tossing his trident to

Delphin as he passed by. He could have climbed the steps on either side of it, but he vanished instead, to hide the grimace that overtook his face when the old sea daemon nearly crumbled under its weight.

He reappeared centerstage a moment later, the perfect image of poise and confidence. At least that's what he hoped. He felt quite the opposite and his mood darkened even as he put an arm over his midsection and bowed. This whole thing had become a spectacle.

"Ladies, would you care to join me, please?" he said, tamping down the urge to bellow at them all—Nereus and Doris, their court, even Delphin—in frustration.

CHAPTER 10

Amphitrite watched with rapt interest from the wings as Poseidon held out his hand to dark-haired, coral-eyed Thetis as she stepped onto the stage. She looked like a young girl next to him, as they all did compared to his towering size. But Thetis was no girl. She was one of the oldest nereids, born with skin as well as scales. She could morph into many creatures, both land and sea, but today gills slashed her neck, and a sleek shark fin ran down her spine. Amphitrite had always admired Thetis's unique gift, but not this day. The pale gray skin and rows of sharply pointed teeth made her sister appear as though she were more predator than nereid, and it was unnerving.

It was no secret Thetis was infatuated with the gods, to the point of obsession. Perhaps the dangerous beauty she possessed was the reason she felt she belonged among them and not below. Yet, if glowering was her way of aligning herself with the gods she wanted to live among, Amphitrite found her sister's indifferent demeanor to be a curious choice.

It wasn't unexpected, exactly, but she thought Thetis might have considered projecting more of a beaming eagerness than a cold aloofness when given the opportunity to become what she longed for most—a goddess. Instead, she gave the impression she was not inspired by the idea in the slightest. It seemed she was going off the assumption that an Olympian would want what he could not have, which certainly aligned with her imperious nature.

Amphitrite shuddered, unable to imagine being that cold or callous... or calculating.

The dance ended with Thetis offering King Poseidon nothing but a curt nod before walking off as though she had just finished dancing with the court jester. All eyes remained on the King, including Amphitrite's. They held their breath, waiting to see how he would react. An impatient roar? An earthquake? A tidal wave?

A collective sigh of relief filled the room when he simply smiled and gestured for the next of them to come forward. It was assumed they would go in the order they were announced, but Galatea did not move. Before Amphitrite could think of imparting an encouraging word, Calypso shoved Galatea out onto the stage. She stumbled from the force, which had been harder than necessary, before slowly walking toward the smiling King. Amphitrite shot Calypso a harsh look, but of course she refused to acknowledge it.

Amphitrite returned her focus to Galatea, noticing that by the time she reached King Poseidon, she was trembling. Despite this, he gently took her hands in his and they began to dance. They moved in awkward silence for a while, the room silent save for the music.

They continued this way until the King stopped and took her chin in his hand, lifting her gaze so that she looked at him when he spoke. The musicians played softer in the hope they could hear what he had to say.

Tears streamed down Galatea's pale and stricken face, with her only nodding or shaking her head occasionally. After a few minutes of one-sided conversation, King Poseidon placed a hand on each of Galatea's shoulders. He said one last thing to her, causing her tear swollen eyes to widen. Dropping her head into her hands, she turned away and quickly left the dance floor.

Amphitrite glanced at Doris, to gauge her mother's reaction. Doris's face remained placid, but Amphitrite knew there was fury churning just below the calm surface. Galatea would surely suffer the consequences of making Doris, and herself, look senseless and weak.

But Amphitrite had seen the small smile on Galatea's face before she'd hidden it behind her fingers. That small tip of Galatea's lips, the relief in them, proved to Amphitrite the rumor was true. Galatea was in love with a mortal. As such, she had successfully removed herself from the running to be queen.

Poor Galatea. What could she do if she was destined to fall in love with a mortal? One does not go against the Fates. That would be as futile as swimming against a powerful current.

King Poseidon had reacted calmly, confirming something else to Amphitrite. He was capable of something much more valuable than passion. He possessed sympathy. There had been no point in continuing the dance with Galatea, everyone could see that, and he had accepted it with decorum. Although he must have been offended, it wasn't lost on Amphitrite how graciously he had let Galatea go.

Calypso strutted out before Galatea could even make it to the side of the stage. This did not surprise Amphitrite, and she opened her arms to Galatea to offer her sister comfort.

"Everything is going to be all right," whispered Amphitrite, resisting the urge to roll her eyes at the sight of Calypso's exaggerated curtsy centerstage.

"But mother will never allow..." began Galatea.

"Hush, sweet sister," replied Amphitrite. "We cannot help who we love. The road ahead will be difficult, but you are stronger than you know."

Galatea nodded, sniffling as Amphitrite released her so she could wipe away her tears. She desperately wanted to ask Galatea what King Poseidon had said, but she did not think it would be courteous to do so when her sister's eyes were not yet dry.

The pair began the dance, Calypso taking command of the conversation right away. Amphitrite could hardly bear to watch her sister as she made the King smile and laugh with her wit and charm. Amphitrite knew it was calculated, as everything Calypso did was.

It's just as well. Even if he were to choose me, I cannot accept.

How could she? She was an ordinary nereid. Besides, too many of them needed her here—her sisters, her friends at the reef, the creatures of the deep—not off in some shining royal palace.

When the dance between King Poseidon and Calypso ended, Amphitrite found herself wishing she had a few more minutes. She had been shocked when he'd called her name. Hadn't she purposely foregone adornments, choosing instead to let the others shine brighter than she? Still, here she was, about to dance with the King of the Sea anyway.

And it would all be for nothing.

As expected, Calypso glared at her as she exited, the reminder not to outdo her clear. Amphitrite's chest tightened. One dance, that was it, then it would be over. Calypso could have her way and Amphitrite could go back to taking care of those she loved.

CHAPTER 11

Poseidon usually had more command over his limbs than he did now. His body had gone as taut as a bowstring, leaving every muscle drawn tight. Over a single dance with a nereid? Nymphs had no power to speak of, and they wielded no weapons. Unless, of course, long golden tresses could be considered armaments. By the way he trembled merely being close to this alluring creature, it seemed they could. Clearly, this was no ordinary circumstance and Amphitrite was no ordinary nymph.

Could Delphin be right? Had the Fates led him here, to her?

After he bowed and she curtsied, as was customary, they each stepped forward and took the other's hands. Her fingers were small compared to his, and so delicate he made sure to keep his grip loose, careful not to crush them with the hope she would find him desirable.

Or at least *likeable.*

He smiled down at her as they began the series of small slides and soft stomps of the couple's dance. There was a shy smile on her lips, but she said nothing. He should be the first to speak, he knew, but what to say? Whatever it was, it needed to be now.

"Why barnacles?"

She tilted her head in confusion, her silky rose gold waves falling across her collarbone, but before he could fully admire the sight, she spoke, drawing his attention back to her deep blue eyes.

"Every life is important, Your Majesty. Even those that seem dull deserve a chance to show their true brilliance."

He wanted to laugh out loud, but not to ridicule or shame her. She had offered a different perspective, a view so refreshing in its simplicity that it had genuinely surprised him. It delighted him to no end, in fact, and he might even go so far as to say it warmed his heart to her even more.

"So, while the others chose extravagant ways to get my attention," he said, careful not to glance at Calypso, "you don't wish for it at all?"

"That is not exactly true, but I suppose if that is how you choose to see it," replied Amphitrite. He could not keep his head from tilting, his gaze roaming her face for more explanation. Although he had not meant to be so intense, she took his curiosity as offence, and it made her blush. "I just mean that I have no need for attention. In fact, I am quite the opposite. I find great joy in letting others shine."

Poseidon nodded. "That's why you helped your sister, the one who was failing miserably at dancing."

Amphitrite's gaze snapped to his. "Yes, and I would do it again, no matter what the consequence."

Her eyes glittered with hard resolve, and it gave him hope there was more to her than just a humble heart. If she were to be his queen, she would also need a strong spine.

"And would you find joy in taking care of a king?" asked Poseidon.

"If a king needed taking care of, then yes. But I should hope he would learn to help himself," she said before meeting his gaze once again. "For the sake of his kingdom *and* his queen."

Poseidon's heart jumped in his chest. He knew exactly her meaning. His outbursts, she would expect him to try harder to curb them. Part of him balked at this unspoken stipulation. He was an Olympian, one who'd defeated many a Titan in the long war for supremacy with the very temper she was referring to now.

But the other part of him was abashed.

Although he knew how his tempestuous nature must affect the inhabitants of the sea whenever his anger flared—he had seen the aftermath of it when great whales had been flung onto the shore to their deaths—he hadn't given it much thought. It rose in him a strange mix of emotion, one he did not know how to navigate, and so he avoided its uncomfortableness all together and steered the conversation elsewhere.

He cleared his throat.

"What would you do as queen?" he asked. Then, thinking the question might reveal too much, he added, "Should you be chosen, of course."

She replied almost as soon as the words left his mouth. "Whatever it took to protect every creature from their King's temper."

Normally, his anger would rise when challenged like this, even as gentle as it was, but Poseidon found himself conceding. She was right. A king *should* have his subjects' best interest at heart, not only in words but in deeds as well, protecting them and not simply ruling over them.

Zeus had been right in suggesting he take a wife; he could see the wisdom in it now. Delphin had been right, too, and Poseidon was never so grateful he had remained open to the possibility The Fates might show him favor. Agreeing to choose one of Nereus's daughters had been a vital step toward his destiny, one he almost did not take. But he had, and one dance with this nymph, both gentle and stern in her convictions, was all it took to finally give him a purpose to temper his passion.

But he didn't feel as though it was being forced. He wanted to, for her.

Pleasure and pain were sure to come along with making her happy, but he was willing to endure it, for he had gone looking for the perfect wife and he had found her.

CHAPTER 12

The music ended, and Poseidon stifled a groan of disappointment. He could have continued his conversation with Amphitrite all night, but the dance was over. The saving grace was, after their wedding tomorrow, they would have the rest of their days to talk.

He bowed at the same time she curtsied. Still holding onto her hands, he pictured her by his side always, and he felt compelled to lift one to his lips and kiss the delicate skin there.

But he refrained. He hadn't done the same for the others and doing such a thing now would give his true feelings away. He must practice patience.

Once Poseidon had reluctantly let go of Amphitrite so she could join her sisters at the side of the stage, he nodded at Delphin to bring him his trident. Always at the ready, Delphin rushed forward with it. He held it with both hands, barely able to lift it as he stumbled up the steps. Poseidon reached out a hand and called it to him before his old friend hurt himself.

The weight of it was a comfort. He'd felt vulnerable without it, but now, with his mighty symbol of power back in his grip, he felt confident and ready to make his announcement.

Although he had found Galatea gentle and sweet, she was hopelessly in love with another. A man named Acis, she'd confessed. He hadn't had the heart to tell her love affairs with mortals never led to anything good. Unlike her sisters Calypso and Thetis, who were all tooth and claw, Amphitrite had not grated on his nerves, but soothed them.

There had been no choice in the matter, really.

Poseidon tapped the end of his trident on the stage thrice, signaling he was about to address the court. He gestured with his free hand for the four nereids to rejoin him.

"I have made my choice."

He should have kept Amphitrite from having to leave only to immediately return. This elaborate show of ceremony was scrambling his wits as well as draining his patience.

One by one the nereids appeared from the wings, Calypso, of course, rushing to his side first. Oh, how badly he wanted to throttle her. Instead, he somehow found the strength to keep the annoyance from his face, waiting until they were all there before speaking.

He would say something positive about the three he did not choose, to soften the blow of disappointment they would surely feel. Although, considering Thetis's indifferent stare and Galatea's relieved smile, both in contrast to the confident way Calypso's chin tipped upward, only one of them might be upset.

Not wanting to draw out the agony for any longer than he needed to—it had already gone on long enough—Poseidon turned toward Thetis. It was only right to address each nereid directly instead of speaking as though they were not there.

"Thetis. I appreciate your unique power and beauty," began Poseidon, "but I'm afraid your countenance leaves me cold." To no one's surprise, Thetis did not react. "Galatea. You are as lovely and delicate as a flower," he continued, "but you are too fragile for a brute like me. I wish you well." He winked at her, and when she mouthed the words *thank you* he nodded. "Calypso. If it weren't for you, I would not have gotten the chance to know for certain who among you would please me most." Calypso's smile was smug, and it needled at him. "Your ambition will take you far... but not to my palace."

He bit the inside of his cheek to keep from smiling when her mouth dropped open.

The hall remained as silent as the dead. Not a single member of the court blinked out of fear the moment they had all been waiting for would pass them by. With his heart hammering in his chest, he turned toward the nymph with the sunset in her hair.

"Amphitrite." He inhaled, not knowing how to sum up all he felt in so few words. "Your grace and beauty precede you..." Poseidon tried to catch her gaze, but she was staring down at her feet, worrying one end of her hair between nervous fingers. He stepped toward her, lifting her chin and pulling her face upward until their eyes met. "Your warm and caring nature elevate you." He had barely known what to say with the others, but with Amphitrite, once the words poured out of him, he found he could not stop them from flowing.

"My tumultuous nature is no secret." He let go of her chin to take her hands in his. "But with you by my side, I believe I could finally take command of it." The color drained from her face, making his heart stutter. It would be no small task to be his queen, he would admit that, but hadn't he made it clear he would try? He would be different with her, yet she still looked unsure, which made his confidence falter, the stricken look on her face causing his breath to hitch. "Or at least control it better."

His audience was captive, waiting with bated breath for the King of the Sea to stop his love-struck rambling and say aloud which beloved daughter of Nereus he had chosen. Even though, he suspected they already knew.

The only one in the entire hall he cared about was Amphitrite. But she did not speak, only stared up at him with an expression on her face he could not read.

"I choose you, Amphitrite," he said. Then, instead of declaring she was his, it felt only right to ask her if she *wanted* to be, instead of being forced. "Will you be my bride?"

CHAPTER 13

Amphitrite's stomach dropped when the shouts and cheers exploded around her. She glanced over just in time to witness the shocked expression on Calypso's face turn into a bitter sneer. Then, just as quickly, her lips smoothed themselves into a feigned smile of congratulations.

Thetis continued to stare ahead icily while Galatea clutched her chest in relief. All Amphitrite could do was stand there, frozen, feeling as though she might faint. Galatea placed a reassuring hand on her back, and Amphitrite was thankful her reaction was far more gracious than Calypso's had been.

The announcement had elicited a reaction from them all, for entirely different reasons, but the one that plagued Amphitrite with guilt the most was Calypso's. Amphitrite had the thing she wanted, and, just as Calypso had feared, Amphitrite had won it without even trying.

Amphitrite knew it would not be her that paid for this, but Galene. The timid girl was already a target when it came to Calypso's jeering taunts and cruel games, and with

Amphitrite not there to protect her, she would most certainly be subjected to worse.

Amphitrite's head spun, causing her to sway unsteadily. She wanted to crumple to the floor and weep, but that seemed more like something Calypso would do, so she steeled herself. Through sheer willpower she managed to remain upright as her sisters hastily exited the stage.

Poseidon held a smaller trident. Where or how he'd gotten it, she didn't know. He must have conjured it out of thin air. The thought of possessing that much power made the edges of Amphitrite's vision go dark.

"Congratulations, my dear," said Nereus. "Now accept the gift from your betrothed."

Her father's command was not harsh, and she tried to obey, but she could not coax her arms nor her legs to move. Yet, her head shook with no difficulty, betraying her and exposing her trepidation.

"No. No... There's been a m-mistake," she stuttered, as though willing a different outcome into existence with words alone were possible.

"A mistake?" said King Poseidon, stunned.

Amphitrite looked up, wincing at the way his furrowed brow contorted his handsome face before, in the blink of an eye, he regained his composure. His broad chest expanded into an impossibly large wall of muscle, and she sank into herself, her eyes lowering back down to the ground as she waited for the angry outburst that was surely to come.

But the room remained utterly still, one second turning into several, ticking by until a full minute of silence had passed.

"Look at me, Amphitrite," said King Poseidon.

It was more of a plea than a command, and like a moth to a flame, she could not help herself from doing what he asked.

"I assure you, I have made no mistake," he said gently. "I choose you."

Overwhelmed, Amphitrite squeezed her eyes shut. She had thought she did not want marriage, wanting instead to remain free of the burden for all her days. After her dance with the King of the Sea, something had changed. It seemed not only for her, but him as well. He had spoken with such ease and sincerity it made Amphitrite feel both special and riddled with guilt at once. She felt sorry for Galene and the others, even Calypso with all her scheming and conniving ways, because, deep down, she'd *wanted* him to choose her.

With tears threatening to spill from her eyes, Amphitrite fled from the hall. The astounded gasps and loud murmurs echoed loudly, and it was more than she could bear, but she refused to let her emotions get the best of her. She held in her tears as she ran, throwing off her diadem as she ran down the corridor and unleashing a cry of dismay when she reached her room.

She slammed the door shut and whirled around to press her back against it. Only then, with her head in her hands, did she let her tears fall.

She wished he would have chosen Calypso and saved them—and her—the trouble. There was no way her sister was going to go along with this quietly. She would do everything in her power to make everyone around her suffer. How was Amphitrite supposed to live with that knowledge?

She couldn't, and so she would refuse the marriage.

She fell to her knees and, clasping her hands, prayed to the only deities more powerful than Poseidon, even than Zeus himself. The Fates.

"Clotho, Lachesis, Atropos, sentinels of fate and keepers of destiny, I beseech you to remove me from Poseidon's heart," she whispered.

A knock sounded at the door.

"Amphitrite. Open the door."

Her mother. Amphitrite reached up and unlatched the lock as quickly as her fumbling fingers would allow. She rose to her feet and opened the door.

Doris strode into the room, whirling around once she reached its center. Her attendants began to straighten her skirts, but she ordered them to leave, the sternness of her voice sending them clambering over one another. Once they were gone, and the door closed, she spoke.

"It is a great honor Poseidon has chosen you to be his queen," she began. "Why do you shame your family with this show of impertinence?"

Amphitrite tugged on the ends of her hair, not wanting to place the blame on Calypso but feeling as though she had no other option. "I'm sorry. I mean no dishonor, but it is better for us all if the King takes Calypso as his queen. She is the stronger match."

"How so?"

"She is bold." *She desperately wants out of here.* "And she is driven." *And she will stop at nothing to leave.* "To the point of ill treatment of others. If she does not get her way, the whole castle will be miserable."

Doris remained silent. What was there left to say? Amphitrite had answered her without mincing words. Finally, after what seemed like an eternity, Doris shook her head as she turned toward a window.

"As much as I would like to disagree, I'm afraid you are right. Calypso is quite ambitious." She placed a hand on the stone, bracing herself as she peered out into the ocean. "She needs so much... but there are so many of you... and we... Nereus and I cherish all of you, of course, but I cannot help but feel as though we have somehow made the insatiable void inside Calypso's restless heart deeper."

Doris sighed wearily, the sound of it making Amphitrite's heart ache. She hadn't embraced her mother since she was a small girl, but she stepped closer, wanting desperately to wrap her arms around her mother's shoulders. But before she could, Doris slipped back into place as stoic Titan goddess, turning away from the window to face Amphitrite once more.

"No, mother. You have not failed her. Nor have I," said Amphitrite, abandoning any notion of a warm embrace. Her mother found comfort in the truth, however bitter it may be, and so Amphitrite would offer a solution instead. "It is simply her self-aggrandizing nature at play. We must allow her this or we will all suffer. If you or I deny her what she wants, she will destroy us with a thousand tiny cuts."

"And you think it wise to allow her to fail Poseidon?"

"She will not fail him," replied Amphitrite, taking a step back. "She will rule him fiercely, love him passionately... obsessively. An Olympian god must be worshiped, do they not?"

Her mother blinked at her, saying nothing. Then, after a few agonizing moments, she nodded her head, confirming what they both knew what needed to be done.

"You cannot stay here," said Doris, her eyes glassy with unshed emotion. "You must hide until they are wed and gone."

CHAPTER 14

Poseidon had been stunned into silence. He had chosen Amphitrite, but she had refused him. Worse, she had done so in front of her father's entire court, humiliating him.

"Retrieve her," Nereus had ordered his wife when it was apparent Amphitrite did not simply need a few moments to collect herself.

Doris had pursed her lips and sent him a cold stare, but she had not moved.

Poseidon had recognized the indignation. Commands didn't set well with him either. He hadn't wanted to make the proud old sea nymph comply with her husband's command, but his want for Amphitrite's retrieval had been greater. Neither Thetis or Calypso had captured his heart and mind like their sister had, and so Poseidon had nodded at Doris, reissuing her husband's missive. As expected, she had relented and rose to her feet.

And now it seemed she had been gone for an eternity.

A heavy feeling had sunk into the pit of his stomach as he'd made his way back to the royal table and sat down. Nereus's court had witnessed something they would never see again.

An Olympian humbled.

The terrible thought still taunted him as he sat waiting impatiently. His embarrassment continued to mount until he heard the crunch of shell. He willed himself to loosen his ferocious grip on the mother of pearl goblet. It took all the strength he had to resist the urge to throw it at Nereus. Instead, he hid his other hand beneath the table and balled it into a tight fist.

Everything within him wanted to flip the table, send its contents asunder, choke the life out of the old Titan instead of merely throwing a cup at him, but the words Amphitrite had spoken earlier came to mind.

I should hope he would learn to help himself... for the sake of his kingdom and his queen.

As the minutes approached half of an hour's time since Doris had left the hall, the court remained silent, no doubt waiting anxiously to see if he would lose all patience and storm after her to retrieve her himself. The way they cowered on the edge of their seats waiting for his tirade to begin annoyed him, but he was determined to remain calm.

Finally, Nereus spoke. "My good people, have no fear. Amphitrite is simply overwhelmed." He glanced in the direction in which his daughter had fled. "I have every confidence our beloved queen will calm her nerves. Meanwhile, let us continue our merriment, for one way or another, there will be a wedding tomorrow morning!"

He lifted a cup in the air with one hand, signifying the musicians should continue playing. Once the music began again, he turned toward Poseidon.

"Have patience, Your Majesty. All will be well. If Amphitrite still refuses, I have forty-nine other daughters who will not."

Have patience? Had the old Titan implied Poseidon had none? He had shown plenty of restraint already. The dining hall still stood, after all. Did Nereus truly have no idea the enormous effort it had taken—was *still* taking—not to destroy everything and everyone around him?

Poseidon willed away the urge to slam his fists into the table and nodded instead. The last thing he wanted to do was frighten Amphitrite any further.

Or destroy her home.

"You are a true ally, Nereus. Now enjoy yourself," he said, lifting his own cup and repeating Nereus's sentiment. "All will be well."

He couldn't help but regret the words as soon as they left his mouth. All would not be well. Not for him, at least. It was plain Amphitrite did not want to be the wife of a tyrant. Could he blame her? He had been careless in his anger over the years. So much so that his reputation as a violent and uncaring ruler had preceded him.

He lifted his hand for more wine and a cupbearer hurried over. He smiled as she poured, nodding at her cheerfully as though his insides were not roiling. As though a truly terrible thought wasn't forming in his mind. He might have to marry one of the others. Not Galatea, obviously, but Thetis or Calypso.

"Shall I go see if I can be of assistance somehow?" said Delphin.

If it were possible an Olympian could be startled, Poseidon would have flinched. He'd been so lost in his thoughts he had forgotten Delphin had been there at all. He shook his head, determined to remain hopeful.

"Let's wait and see," said Poseidon somberly.

He should have known The Fates would do this to him. Bringing him this close to contentment only to snatch it away. If Doris did not show up with Amphitrite, he would be forced to settle. He bit the inside of his lip as he wrestled his panic into submission. He had neither the time nor the inclination to prolong his search for a wife.

Poseidon drank his wine, watching the court continue their celebrations as though they had already forgotten his complete and total mortification. He supposed he was glad for it, yes, but it did nothing to ease the sting he'd felt when Amphitrite had run from the room. It had felt like he had taken an arrow to the heart. No, a sword. It felt as though she had taken something he hadn't even known he'd wanted.

Now, as Doris returned to the hall alone, he felt rejected all over again.

The court's laughter quieted to murmurs when Doris approached the dais. She pulled out her chair and sat, speaking in a low voice so only Nereus and Poseidon could hear.

"I'm afraid Amphitrite is gone."

"Gone?" echoed Nereus.

Poseidon did not trust his mouth to speak. How could he? Both hands were openly curled into fists now and his jaw was clenched. He had known there was a chance he would find himself in this position, but until now, until this very moment, he'd been holding out hope Amphitrite would change her mind.

"Gone," repeated Doris. "My attendants and I have searched everywhere. She has fled the castle."

The sea around them swayed, even though Poseidon tried to keep the water still, his temper had a mind of its own. It took several seconds to regain control of it, but when he finally did, he tried to keep the condescension from his voice. "Where has she gone *to*?"

Doris blanched, but still managed to keep a small modicum of calm as she answered. "I don't know, Your Majesty."

When her face turned as gray as an eel, Poseidon knew she was sick with panic, and desperately praying the situation would not go from bad to worse, perhaps even turning deadly.

For reasons he could not understand, he felt ashamed at this, so, feeling like a simpering fool, he forced himself to continue as though unbothered.

"No matter. As your husband has said..." He turned to Nereus and clapped him on the shoulder. "There are forty-nine others."

True enough, but he didn't want them. He longed for Amphitrite. But what could he do if she did not feel the same? Under different circumstances, he might have forced her to comply.

But that was before this day.

Would he regret marrying another? Perhaps, but he couldn't think of that now. He must do what he came here to do. All he wanted was for the night to be over. It was taking every ounce of strength he had not to get up and go to his room where he could be alone.

If missing someone before you even got to know them made him feel this miserable, then perhaps this was for the best. Reminded why he had not wanted to marry in the first place, he held up his cup for more wine.

"You must choose another," whispered Doris. "I am quite sure Calypso would be happy to be your queen."

A tempest of emotions—anger, frustration, despair—whirled inside of him, but the one he chose to show was apathy. And so, he nodded in agreement.

CHAPTER 15

Poseidon sat on the top of a cliff, arms resting on his knees as he stared out at the sunrise. He'd come here to soak in the rose-tinged brilliance that reminded him so much of the nymph he thought he would be marrying this morning.

He suspected he would come to a spot like this often, to contemplate how and why his quest for a wife had gone so terribly wrong. Nothing like this had happened to him before, and he struggled to make sense of why it was happening now. He might have the answer one day, but for now, he would have to be content with wondering how it was possible to long for someone you only just met the day before.

The thought boggled his mind. He was a god. Despite this, he had heard the whispers that some of his divine brethren had been smitten in even less time. In some cases, like Apollo and Daphne, it was upon first sight. It was true the God of Love, Eros, and one of his leaden arrows were rumored to be the reason Apollo pined after the nymph, but Poseidon didn't dignify the existence of lesser gods like Eros often, let alone that they held such power. He had on the other hand, seduced Eros's mother on more than one occasion. Had Aphrodite's son struck him with one of his arrows, to stop the advances toward his mother?

Anything was possible, he supposed, but the affair was in the past, over and done with. It was more likely the Fates were the culprits.

He looked out at the horizon, imagining swimming into it with Amphitrite by his side. Instead, he was alone, with his thoughts swirling around his mind as fast and as furious as a funnel cloud. Was he simply feeling sorry for himself for being denied something he wanted? That was part of it, he couldn't excuse that away, but the bigger truth of it was he'd been taken with Amphitrite from the moment he had laid eyes on her. And then he had fallen deeper in love with every word she'd spoken.

On the heels of that came another thought. He had been right all along, and how the Fates must be laughing. He had tempted them by daring to go out and find a woman who completed him instead of following the destiny they had set for him. As punishment, they had seen to it he could think of nothing or no one else.

No, they did not favor him, and now he sat on the hard ground, love struck like a common man, feeling utterly foolish for thinking they ever had.

Poseidon raked his fingers through his hair. In a few hours, he would stand before Nereus's court and recite empty vows, marrying a woman who was, in his mind, nothing more than a means to an end. He stood, narrowing his eyes at the sky before diving headlong into the waves.

When he arrived back at Nereus's castle, it was bustling with activity. He had intended to go straight to his room, but soon found himself lost. How many nooks and crannies could one castle have? And why were so many needed? He laughed at his hypocrisy, thinking how his own palace had three times the rooms.

He quickened his pace. Delphin would be in a panic by now, thinking he'd broken his promise and returned to his golden palace. To be honest, the thought had crossed his mind, but he did not wish for "oath breaker" to replace "earth shaker."

Thoroughly lost, he followed the sound of voices up ahead, intending to ask whoever it was if they would be so kind as to point him in the right direction back to his room. When he reached the door, he was surprised it was cracked and not closed. Peering inside, he saw Calypso surrounded by several attendants, all pulling and tugging at some part of her.

He was about to turn and leave when the nereid lashed out, slapping one of them hard across the face.

Calypso did not see him, but Doris, who was there to oversee the dressing of her daughter, did. Their eyes met, and Poseidon held her gaze, considering whether to announce his presence or quietly walk away. As their King, it was well within his right to step in and reprimand both his bride-to-be and her mother. The former for such crude and unbecoming behavior, and the latter for allowing it to happen.

He didn't get the chance. Doris strode across the room without a word and slipped out into the corridor, closing the door behind her.

She swallowed hard before speaking. "She is plagued with nerves."

Poseidon did not counter. What could he say? It was as though someone had held a mirror up to him. And he hadn't liked what he'd seen. It reminded him of the excuses that his brother Zeus had used countless times to defend him when the other Olympians lodged a complaint against some perceived offense he had committed.

Usually it wasn't perceived at all, but well and truly real, done with malice and spite.

"I know she was not your first choice," said Doris.

"Nor my second."

She inhaled deeply, attempting to keep herself collected. "You will grow to love—" She stopped herself. "Appreciate her determination."

"Will I?" Or would it fuel his fire and turn him into a more violent and unpredictable dictator?

The cold calmness dropped from Doris's face, and the worried creases left behind revealed she knew marrying Calypso would only make his temper worse, a truth which did not bode well for any of them.

"I truly hope so," she said. "Come, I will show you back to your room. The hour draws near."

Later, when Calypso stood before him looking innocent and sweet, the scene from earlier flashed behind his eyes, reminding him she was anything but. It caused the burning sensation in his stomach to move to his chest before slowly turning into a sharp pain that stabbed at his temples.

He tried loosening his clenched jaw, but it was no use. He knew without a shadow of a doubt that Calypso would only stoke his fiery temper, making it worse than it already was.

"Poseidon?" said Calypso from beneath her veil.

His gaze snapped to hers. Who did this nereid think she was? She was not yet a queen. Was she so bold to think it would be wise to address him by the name given to him by his parents and not as her King?

Delphin, who stood close, put a hand on his shoulder. "My Lord," he said. "Do you need a moment?"

Poseidon's nostrils flared. The only thing he needed was to find Amphitrite, so that he could prove to her... what, exactly? That he'd pretended he didn't care when she left? That their connection had been a sham, just like the ceremony that was to take place here in her father's court, so he could leave it with a wife on his arm?

It was a formality. Their empty vows would need to be repeated in the presence of Zeus and the others to make them binding. And with every fiber of his being, he did not want to be bound to Calypso. Not when Amphitrite existed in the world.

What would Zeus do, if he were in Poseidon's current position? Would he marry a woman he did not want because the one he truly wanted had run away? It wasn't even a question. If Zeus could marry everyone, he would.

But Poseidon was not like his brother. His heart belonged to one woman only.

"I will not do this," he said. "I chose Amphitrite, and if she will not have me, I shall take no other."

Calypso ripped the veil from her face, her eyes darting between him and Doris. "Amphitrite ran away because she does not want you!"

Fury burned hot in Poseidon's face. He gripped his trident harder, calling his power into action. The trident glowed, ready to do his bidding.

He narrowed his eyes, glaring at Doris with open contempt. "Your daughter dares address your King in this way?"

"*I* am to be your queen, *not* my sister," insisted Calypso before turning toward Doris. "Mother, you said—"

"Silence, child," warned Doris, stepping closer to Calypso and grasping her upper arm to avert additional offence.

Poseidon scowled at them both, the water beginning to sway, pitching them back and forth as his anger rose.

"Where is Amphitrite?"

"Your Majesty…" began Doris.

"Where is she?" bellowed Poseidon, thoroughly enraged she would not answer his question.

Doris pulled a wailing Calypso to her breast, her face tortured by the decision she faced; betray one daughter by revealing where the other had gone.

"I will ask only once more." Poseidon's trident burned brighter, pulsing with anger.

"The Atlas Mountains," she replied, bowing her head.

Poseidon lifted his trident with a curled lip and flared nostrils, unable to contain his fury at being lied to. Moreover, that Amphitrite had been skillfully strummed like a lyre, lured into the trap of her conniving sister.

"Step aside, Doris," he commanded. "Lest you wish to perish with your daughter."

Calypso let out a frightened cry.

"Careful, My Lord," Delphin intervened, just in time. "If you do what I think you are about to do, you may never get Amphitrite back. Let me find her, bring to her a proposition. I shall tell her the truth of your heart, and the mercy you have shown toward her family here today."

A low growl emanated from Poseidon. Delphin was right, yet again.

So was Amphitrite. *Every life is important, Your Majesty.*

Poseidon sighed, releasing his outrage and allowing empathy to take its place.

"She must be punished for her insolence," he replied, his irritation subsiding. "But thanks to the wisdom of others, she will not die this day." He fixed his gaze on the nereid who caused those around her to needlessly suffer. "You drove your sister away from me, and so you shall be driven away yourself." He lifted his trident, ready to deliver a sentence more just than he thought she deserved. "I banish you to the island of Ogygia, to live out the rest of your days alone, just as you sought to do to another."

"No! Please don't—"

But before she could finish her cry for mercy, Poseidon tapped his trident and Calypso vanished.

CHAPTER 16

Amphitrite had raced to the furthest reaches of the sea, swimming until she had arrived at her destination, bedraggled and exhausted. In those first few hours, it had seemed as though she would never get to the mountains, but she'd kept going, determined to put as much distance between the confusion and guilt plaguing her as she could. Except, she hadn't outrun either of them. They were still there, gnawing at her heart and weighing down her mind.

She'd cried the whole way, her hot tears flowing into the cold sea, swimming until she could barely move, but she had dragged herself to shore anyway. Blessedly, she hadn't had to search for long before finding a small alcove in which to rest.

Her back had sagged against the rocky cave wall as she'd shivered for hours. Finally, after her tears had subsided, she had laid down and closed her eyes, willing sleep to come. Her relentless thoughts had kept her mind awake until, after what seemed like forever, she'd fallen asleep.

It had only been a day or two since Amphitrite fled that horrible scene, but, in some ways, it felt as though it had been a lifetime. The water around her remained calm, almost eerily so, and to say this surprised her would be an understatement. She had expected the sea to crash against itself in constant and merciless rage at her rejection of King Poseidon. She still couldn't believe what she had done. She couldn't imagine it was very often anyone refused him.

If she was being honest with herself, she hadn't cried because she didn't know how long she'd have to be away from her family, though, that was most certainly true, nor the embarrassment of it all. She wept because she felt ashamed of how much she had wanted to be chosen.

She told herself lies to keep her from crying anew. The glances and the earnest way he had stared at her, willing her to look into his eyes, meant nothing. The conversation they had shared, and the gentle way he had spoken to her, as if he had been interested in knowing the secrets of her heart, had been a ruse.

He was an Olympian, after all, with a notorious reputation for being arrogant and churlish. They could be as malevolent as they were benevolent. One had only to listen to the stories of trickery and revenge to know that. He had been seeking a marriage of convenience, and not a wife to cherish and treat as an equal. It had been nothing more than that, and they had all been fooled, especially Calypso.

Amphitrite frowned every time she thought about her. Even after all she had done, Amphitrite couldn't bear to think of the devastation that would surely befall her sister when she realized she truly had not escaped at all.

Sadness overtook her, and she curled her limbs into her middle tighter, hugging her own warmth to her like a child keeping a cherished toy safe. It would be weeks, perhaps months, before she could go home again. In the meantime, she would get to know the creatures in this part of the sea. There were so many she had never seen before, especially on land, and that was the bright side on which she must look. She would be an ambassador, she decided, for both her father and the King, sharing the good news that the latter had found a queen.

She yawned, ignoring the rough edges of rock biting into her side and sinking into the thought that it could have—should have—been her.

Amphitrite woke to the sound of a man's voice. It sounded familiar, though she could not quite place it.

"Oh, thank the Fates!" he exclaimed. "I've finally found you."

She clambered backward, scraping her hands and legs in the process. She blinked at the man with bleary eyes. He had the features of a dolphin.

"W-who are you?" she stammered.

"Oh heavens, am I that unmemorable?" he said, sounding disappointed. "Well, I guess compared to His Majesty..."

Her eyes widened when she remembered. It was the old sea daemon King Poseidon had brought with him to her father's castle. "Delphin?" She pulled her stinging legs up to her chest protectively. "What are you doing here?"

"Oh, come now, don't be frightened," he replied. "I am as harmless as they come. His Majesty has sent me to look for you, so that I might extend you an invitation. And now that I have found you..." He cleared his throat. "You are cordially invited to the palace of King Poseidon and..."

"Queen Calypso?" said Amphitrite testily. "Are you sure it isn't my sister who sends for me?" Honestly, did Calypso possess any grace at all?

"Oh no, definitely not. She's been... well, how do I put this?" said the old sea daemon. "The nereid Calypso won't be making any more demands from now on."

Amphitrite's stomach dropped. "He didn't smite her, did he?" She may not like Calypso, despise her even, but she did not wish ill will to befall her sister, and certainly not death.

"Smite her? Oh, no. Nothing so extreme."

"Then what did he do to his new queen?"

"Why, that's the thing. He did not take her as his queen," replied Delphin. "I mean, he was going to, seeing as how you left in such a hurry."

If the sea daemon had eyebrows, Amphitrite had no doubt they would both be arched. He was leading her.

"What happened?" she asked.

"Well, as you know, His Majesty was expecting to leave your father's castle with a bride."

"What *happened?*" repeated Amphitrite, feeling herself beginning to ruffle.

"She balked a great deal at His Majesty's announcement that he would take no other as his wife, of course. She protested so much that His Majesty... uh... sent her to the far away island of Ogygia. I dare say the whole lot of us were relieved not to be subjected to another word of her lamentation on the matter."

Amphitrite swallowed hard, picturing the scene as Delphin described. Part of her wanted to laugh, wishing she'd been there to witness Calypso's tantrum. The other part of her wanted to cry again, but not out of sadness.

Was this her story? Would they paint it on walls, telling future generations of oceanids how King Poseidon loved her like Oceanus loved Tethys? Would it tell of how he sent a sea daemon to the ends of the Earth to find her because he could not bear to be without her?

Oceanus refused to join the terrible war between the old and new gods to keep his kingdom safe. Could it be fate that his descendant, a nereid with Titan blood should do the same? Except, instead of refusing to join a war, she would agree to marry an Olympian.

Was it her destiny to also have a kingdom to protect?

"I will go with you, but he must prove to me that his intentions are true," she said in a rush, before she thought better of it. "I will ask of him three things."

"Ah, a series of tests!" said Delphin. "Are you sure you're not a goddess, nereid?"

Amphitrite's cheeks flushed at the comparison. She was no goddess. But if she was to become one, she must start thinking like one, especially if she were to be the wife of a powerful god such as Poseidon.

"You cannot tell him." Amphitrite added on the stipulation like a true goddess.

"That's usually how it works." He sent her a conspiratorial grin, but a moment later it faltered. "Although I must point out that you play with fire. What happens if His Majesty is furious at the trickery?"

"He told me that with me by his side he would control his anger," she replied. "If I am to become his queen, I must have this assurance. I must see how he reacts of his own accord. If he finds what I ask of him to be trickery, then I will know the truth of his heart."

CHAPTER 17

Amphitrite gasped when Poseidon's palace finally came into view. It was far bigger than her father's castle. With its many gleaming spires and sprawling size, the scene before her was almost incomprehensible.

She looked at Delphin with wide eyes. "Oh my. It's even grander than I imagined."

The old sea daemon chuckled. "Indeed."

Amphitrite stared up in wonder as they approached the gate. The massive posts on either side—two sirens carved out of lava stone—and its golden pickets shaped like giant three-pointed spears were as intimidating as they were magnificent.

"He will be so pleased you have accepted his invitation." Delphin gestured for her to pass through first. "As I've told you, I have never known him to be so distraught in all my days," he said as they continued toward the portcullis.

Amphitrite shot Delphin another wide-eyed look, this time out of fear. The entrance was barred by two slumbering krakens, their barbed tentacles firmly suckered across the massive doors.

"Ah, well, Olympians are quite extravagant in their displays of power, aren't they?" replied Delphin. "You'll get used to it."

Delphin whistled at the guards. When they did not stir, he tried again, louder, until two pairs of eyes slowly blinked open. Once focused on the intruders before them, menacing growls emanated from them both, so deep and powerful it vibrated the ocean floor.

"Oh, don't be unreasonable," said Delphin, dismissing their upset with a wave of his hand. "It is I, the old sea daemon, Delphin, and this is the lovely nereid Amphitrite." He gestured toward her before urging her to step forward. He huffed as they looked her up and down, inspecting her suspiciously. "His Majesty is expecting us. Come, come! Let us through, and quickly now, before there is a terrible price to pay for the delay."

With that, the krakens loosened their grip on the door and pulled it open.

Even slumped in his throne, the dark circles under his eyes visible from a distance, Poseidon took her breath away. He straightened, sitting upright slowly and blinking as though he could not believe what his eyes were seeing.

"Amphitrite," he whispered, his voice hoarse from disuse. "Is that really you?"

"It is, Your Majesty." She nodded, tugging on the end of the tangled mess of hair draped over her shoulder, even though she told herself she wouldn't. She'd tried to comb it out before Delphin had led her in to see King Poseidon, but it had been a useless endeavor. Just like her resolve to never marry.

"I did not think you would come."

"Your old friend was convincing," she said. "He told me what happened, with Calypso, and that you said if I came back, my every wish would be your command. Is it true?"

"Yes, I will give you anything—"

"No. Is it true that you banished Calypso to an island?"

"It is. I thought it more fitting than... Than what I wanted to do."

"She cannot help it. Something within her is empty. She only seeks to fill the void."

He straightened, raking a hand through his hair before pushing out of his golden chair to make his way toward her.

"You defend her?" he asked as he closed the distance between them, his mood seeming to lighten with every step he took. "Even though she costs many so much?"

"Yes," she replied, her breath catching when she saw how rapidly the dark circles under his eyes vanished, the warm light she had seen at her father's castle coming back into his eyes once more. "She is my sister, and although I may not like the way she carries herself, I am bound by the laws of family to love her."

"You have a kind and gentle heart, Amphitrite," replied Poseidon, now standing before her. "I think it is why Fate has brought us together." He took her hands, his thumbs drawing light lines over her skin. "There is much I can learn from you."

His touch sent a shiver dancing up her spine.

"I think I know why she acts the way she does," said Amphitrite, fighting to stay focused. She must not fall under his spell. At least not yet.

His caresses stilled. "Because she is jealous and petty."

"Yes, I won't deny it," replied Amphitrite, trying to still her wildly beating heart. "But it is because she longs for adoration." It was more than that, though, and so she searched for a more precise explanation. "She needs validation from those around her, to convince herself she is worthy of love."

King Poseidon held her gaze, his face unreadable. After a moment, he nodded. "My first lesson in empathy."

Amphitrite gulped down trepidation. She hadn't meant to draw a comparison between him and Calypso, but it seemed a connection had been made in his mind. Or was it that he was on to her? Had he already figured out she was testing him?

"Not your first." Her words came out in a rush, to fill the silence hanging in the air. "You let Galatea go gracefully."

He chuckled, the sound warm and rich and so deep it reverberated through her. "That's because I already knew who I would be choosing."

His flattery made her cheeks flush deeper.

"Still, your pride must have been wounded."

He shook his head. "No, not then."

She swallowed hard, knowing exactly what he meant. Her leaving cut him deeper than either of them had expected it would, that was plain. But she would contend with that later, right now she needed to see how he reacted to her first request.

"Send someone to the island, to be hers and hers alone."

"Done," Poseidon said without hesitation. "I know just the man."

She glanced at Delphin, who had given them some distance but was still nearby. He tipped his head at her, indicating her first request had been done.

CHAPTER 18

Awe filled Poseidon as they approached a massive coral reef. Sunlight filtered through the water, illuminating it and making it appear as though it were a living mural. While he marveled at the beauty of his domain—one he'd never taken the time to notice—Amphitrite swam towards a sea turtle nestled in the rock. When she urged him closer, he obliged, and after he patted the creature's head with a forefinger, clumsily but gently, he glanced at Amphitrite with a grin. She returned his smile, confirming he'd done well, and his heart soared.

Now that Amphitrite was with him, his thoughts were less brooding, and his mood much lighter. Not only had she brought back his hope, but she had brought back his belief in fate. What she said when she'd first arrived, about her sister needing validation, it was as though she was also speaking about him. Other than it being destiny, he had no idea how she knew his mind so well, understanding the struggle within him so thoroughly. It made him, for the first time, consider how much his actions affected those around him.

And then there was the speed with which she could disarm him—his defenses were crumbling faster than he thought possible. It would be alarming if her presence was not welcomed.

On top of this, she had not been at his palace yet three days and he had found himself wanting to explore every facet of what made him who he was. How was it in just a few days' time she had made him feel so magnanimous? He didn't know how she'd done it, but when she suggested that perhaps he might want to take some time to get to know the creatures he ruled over, he wholeheartedly agreed.

"Do you know of Oceanus?" said Amphitrite amidst of backdrop of brightly colored fish swimming around the coral reef.

"The Titan?" Poseidon nodded, giving the turtle one last pat before straightening. "Yes, I know of him. Why do you ask?"

They continued their meandering tour of the coral and its curious inhabitants. They had come out in droves to meet their king. Or perhaps it was to see *her* again, their soon-to-be queen.

"I am his descendant," she finally replied. "Titan blood flows through my veins."

She was pulling on the ends of her hair. He knew she did this when she was anxious, so he held out his hand to her. It took her a moment to notice, but once she did, she stopped fiddling with her long locks and placed her hand in his.

"If I agree to be your queen," she continued. "Your kingdom will be my kingdom, will it not?" She gestured to the open sea with her free hand. "I will also be responsible for all of this."

What was she getting at? Even if Titan blood did flow through her veins, any children they had together would inherit his kingdom, not her family.

"Well, yes, Amphitrite, that would technically be true, but the Olympians rule now—"

Her huff was barely audible, but it conveyed her frustration loud and clear. "I don't think I am making myself heard. Forgive me for my bluntness, but if I marry you, I must have your word my family remains exempt from any future wars."

Poseidon understood the unwritten rule of family ties. Although often strained, they should never be cut. The Olympians were firmly seated as the prevailing power, but if it came to another battle for supremacy, he would fight to the last breath to protect his family, even Athena.

He stopped walking and reached over to grasp Amphitrite's other hand, turning her toward him so he could look her in the eyes.

"You have my word," he said, squeezing gently to emphasize the sincerity of his words. "If you agree to become my queen, your blood becomes my blood, and I will protect them at all costs."

Her brow remained knitted with uncertainty, causing Poseidon to bite the inside of his cheek. The time had come. He must tell her of his many sons and daughters. A good deal of them had the blood of the old gods coursing through their veins, and he would destroy the world if any of them were to be harmed.

This knowledge could dispel any notion of disloyalty Amphitrite might have, but how could he disclose this without also revealing his indiscretion toward fidelity?

"Amphitrite," he began. "I can assure you that I have no qualms with your Titan blood." He cleared his throat. "Many of my children have Titan mothers."

She was young, but she must know that he had taken lovers before his search for a wife began. He waited for her reaction with clenched teeth.

After a few agonizing seconds, Amphitrite squeezed back, and Poseidon released the breath he'd been holding.

"I believe you," she said, nodding. "And should I accept, I will hold you to it."

Poseidon relaxed, unable to stop a smile from tipping his lips. She was becoming more like a goddess every day, and he could not deny how much this pleased him.

"Come with me to Olympus," he said. Over the last few days, everything she had asked of him was to ensure the protection of her family. It made him appreciate his own. Even with all his many faults, they had never disowned him. "I have met your kin. I would like you to meet mine."

The consternation marring her lovely features vanished, replaced by a smile that set his heart alight. It left no doubt in his mind she was eager to meet his family as he had hers. He only hoped, after all the quarreling he had initiated with is ill-temper, they would still speak highly of him.

CHAPTER 19

A cry of delight nearly escaped her lips, but Amphitrite held it in. She was elated Poseidon had passed every test thus far, but it was the way he opened himself up to her—asking her to meet his family, unprompted—that made her feel as though he could be the Oceanus to her Tethys. But she did not want to seem too eager, so she sent him a bright smile instead.

"I accept," she said, keeping her voice steady. "When shall we go?"

As soon as she asked the question, the fluttering giddiness in her heart turned to a nervous swirling in her belly. The final test, she realized the moment the words left her mouth, would be what his family thought of him. Would they say good things or bad? Would she hear a lament or an exaltation?

"I think there is no better time than the present," he replied. "Come, I will show you the way." He donned a boyish grin before diving backward, the powerful muscles in his arms and legs working in tandem to twist him around and propel him forward.

Amphitrite followed, slicing through the water quickly and nimbly as a seal, swimming by his side until they reached the shore. Excitement flooded through her when they broke the surface. She inhaled, the scent of driftwood and wet rock mingled with the salt air, and a giggle escaped her lips. Poseidon knew her world, but now she would be privy to his.

How she felt now was so far removed from how she'd felt less than a fortnight ago. She'd been ashamed to want all the things she had chastised her sisters for wanting, and here she was, no longer denying that she wanted them, but fully embracing them.

She wasn't sure what it all meant, only that falling in love was the most wonderful feeling in existence.

Helios shined down on them as they walked out of the sea and onto the sandy beach hand in hand. They made their way inland, her on shaky legs and him moving slow and steady until she got used to walking. When they reached the edge of a dense forest at the base of an enormous mountain, Poseidon stopped. He beamed down at her, his jade eyes sparkling as he went to tap his trident on the rocky ground, presumably to whisk them to the top of the mountain.

Amphitrite caught sight of her bare feet, dirty with seaweed and sand. Without thinking, she gripped his forearm.

"Wait!" she cried.

Poseidon's brow creased. "Have you changed your mind?"

"No… it's just…"

He waited patiently for her to continue, but when she failed to get the words out, he reached up and tucked an errant strand of hair behind her ear. His touch was gentle and reverent, with no trace of irritation.

How could this truly be the same god who was notorious for violence?

"Do you worry they won't accept you because you are descended from Titans?" he said softly, caressing her cheek. "I cannot lie, they may be cold at first, but once they know the strength and conviction of your heart, that will not matter. They will be drawn to you as a moth is to a flame."

"It's not that I worry about," she replied, shaking her head.

She looked down at the clothes she wore, dripping with sea water. The scaled bust was molded to her like iridescent fish skin down to her waist, where it morphed into thin strips of kelp, which now clung to her legs in a soggy mess. Her style of dress was practical under the waves, allowing the freedom of movement needed, but Amphitrite felt as though it might not only be too strange looking but also too immodest for the goddesses on Olympus.

Poseidon may be used to the way the sea folk dressed, he might have preferred it even, but there was a very real chance the other Olympians might turn their noses up at the smell of brine and algae that emanated from her and lingered on the air.

"I can't go to Olympus this way." She lifted a strip of the now slimy kelp out for his inspection. "I look—and smell—a fright."

"You are the loveliest thing in all the world, land and sea," he replied. "But if you feel less than beautiful, a change of clothes can be arranged."

Before she could respond he tipped his trident toward her, moving it in a circular motion and calling the ground beneath her feet to funnel up around her.

When it was over, and the whirling cloud of earth had fallen away, she stared down at the jewel encrusted sandals in amazement. She touched her hair, which was now dried into smooth waves and adorned with small clusters of shells. The dress he had conjured for her was unlike anything she had ever seen before. The gauzy pale blue material rippled in the soft sea breeze like waves. She marveled at the way it was draped and pinned at her shoulders with clasps of glittering aquamarine jewels set in gold.

"Thank you," she whispered. "It's beautiful."

"So are you, in every way imaginable," he said, holding out his hand to her. "Shall we?"

She nodded eagerly, barely able to contain her renewed excitement. She slipped her hand into his, and with the tap of his trident, they stood before the gates of Olympus.

CHAPTER 20

Poseidon was relieved when the Olympians remained on their best behavior. Even the notoriously icy Hera had warmed up to Amphitrite, seeming to be just as fascinated as the rest of them. He knew the question on all their minds: How had a lowly nereid managed to capture the King of the Sea's attention so thoroughly?

Like him, it hadn't taken long for them to see that she was anything but a lowly nereid. Her beauty rivaled the likes of theirs, and the deliberate way she spoke, answering their questions and solving their riddles with a quick wit and unshakable confidence, gave them no choice but to welcome her into the divine fray with open arms.

Poseidon leaned against a column and grinned. Once the initial barrage of questions was over, they had gathered to hear Apollo play the lyre as Hermes entertained them by recounting the story of how it was him who'd invented the instrument. He gestured extravagantly, as he always did when he got to the part where he told his captive audience he'd given it to his brother to make amends for stealing his beloved cattle, pristine and white and cherished beyond measure.

Poseidon remembered the squabble between the two young gods well. Apollo had been outraged, to the point he'd gone directly to Zeus, inflicting upon him a rant so long and raving and so loud there left no room for misjudgment of just how angry he was. To hear Hermes tell it now, Apollo had only been mildly irritated. Poseidon chuckled at Hermes' rendition. He'd always been a good storyteller, and it seemed he only got more charming in his delivery as the years passed.

Having never heard the tale before, Amphitrite listened intently, laughing with delight when Apollo rolled his eyes at Hermes' embellishing. It pleased Poseidon to see her this way, at ease among the gods and goddesses of Olympus. In the few days they'd spent getting to know one another, he was learning how important family was to her, how she cherished them—all of them—past and present. Although he and his family quarreled a great deal, he was beginning to appreciate their differences.

Poseidon felt a hand on his shoulder, and a whisper floated up to his ear a moment later.

"She is so tender, Poseidon."

He knew that honey-infused voice anywhere. Aphrodite.

The Goddess of Love slipped her arm around his elbow. "How on Earth did you convince such a lovely creature to marry you?"

His sigh bordered on a huff. "I haven't. Not yet. It was Delphin who convinced her to let me try."

"Ah, so he has appealed to her head." She patted his arm. "Does the powerful and proud Poseidon need help appealing to her heart?"

Poseidon pursed his lips. She was asking him if he wished for her to work her magic on Amphitrite.

"You think me so detestable she would not love me on her own?" he replied.

"Oh, come now, Earth Shaker," she said. "Who understands passion can burn both hot and cold but me?"

"How is Hephaestus?" asked Poseidon, arching a brow at her. He hated being called Earth Shaker. Although he had managed to convince her of his prowess many times, during moments like this, when she playfully taunted him, it still bruised his ego. "I see Ares is here. I assume your husband avoids the truth of your latest affair by staying close to his forge?"

Aphrodite stared at him coolly. "If he would leave his forge once in a while, perhaps his wife would not have to have affairs." Her sapphire eyes sparkled with righteous indignation almost as brightly as the granite surrounding them. "Now, do you love her?" asked Aphrodite, changing the subject.

Poseidon didn't bother to comment that Aphrodite found Hephaestus's lameness undesirable, and that was why she'd strayed. Instead, letting bygones be bygones, his gaze went to his future. Amphitrite.

"Desperately," he replied, not caring if he sounded weak. He did love her. Why pretend otherwise?

Aphrodite tilted her head in reproach. "Love and lust are two different things." She stared at him through long eyelashes. "You do know that?"

Irritation coiled within him. Out of all the Olympians, he had a soft spot in his heart for Aphrodite, but she was trying his patience with her hypocrisy.

"I know the difference, goddess," snapped Poseidon, louder than he'd intended.

"Shhh," said Aphrodite, assuaging his anger with a squeeze to his bicep. "I do not mean to offend you, but if I am to do what you ask of me,

I must be sure you understand what you must give so that you may receive."

"I don't recall asking anything of you," said Poseidon.

"No, not out loud," replied Aphrodite.

Poseidon glanced away. He hadn't, yet somehow the Goddess of Love had known his inner most desire; assurance that there was not only lust in Amphitrite's heart but true, everlasting love.

"I suspect her heart is already open to you, but my magic will see to a long and blissful union." She arched a brow at him. "So long as you keep your mettle in check."

Poseidon's temper flared, fearing he had made too many promises already. "Is that what she wants? Or what you want?"

"Oh, darling." She patted his arm. "It is what every woman wants."

CHAPTER 21

Amphitrite felt more at home in the water, but now that she was used to walking about and breathing air, she inhaled deeply. It was crisp and fresh and full of possibilities, sweetened by the birdsong that could only be heard on land. She adored the sea, in all its dark and mysterious beauty, but she took a moment to appreciate the earth, and the brilliant light that warmed her skin.

She smiled wistfully, having more than one reason to be joyful. The gods and goddesses of Olympus had welcomed her, filling her belly with the finest food and drink while entertaining her with many stories. Best of all, they treated her like one of them. She felt honored, her cheeks warming every time they lavished her with another compliment.

A warm breeze blew, lifting the ends of her hair jauntily as Artemis showed Amphitrite how to hold a bow properly, so her arrows would find their intended target and not a nearby tree. She never imagined herself learning how to shoot an arrow before, but she found it empowering, leaving her feeling as though she could conquer the world.

Or at least protect a kingdom.

After her archery lessons, Aphrodite approached, requesting she join her for a stroll through the gardens.

"I must show you the roses," said Aphrodite. "They are my favorite. Such a symbol of beauty, and they smell divine."

Amphitrite agreed with enthusiasm, eager to know more about the stunning Goddess of Love. They walked along the stone path arm in arm, looking as though they could be sisters. They had the same reddish gold hair, but where Amphitrite's was a waterfall of waves, Aphrodite's fell in the most beautiful cascade of curls. As was to be expected, Aphrodite was taller, with ample hips despite a narrow waist, but Amphitrite's curves held their own next to the goddess's supple shape.

Even though Amphitrite thought her dress, embroidered with gold thread and many precious pearls, made her look regal enough to fit in among the goddesses, it still felt a bit drab next to Aphrodite's billowy white silk cinched by a golden girdle that gleamed almost as brightly as the sun. But Amphitrite didn't dwell on it for long. She was more interested in whether the goddess would have anything to say about the god she was planning to marry.

They made pleasant small talk as they meandered through lush greenery. It was no surprise Aphrodite was an excellent conversationalist. It was easy for Amphitrite to wax poetic about living under the waves, with Aphrodite politely interjecting at the right times to enhance the exchange.

"Did you know that I, too, was born in the ocean?" asked Aphrodite. "From sea foam, more specifically."

Amphitrite's brow furrowed quizzically at that, indicating she wanted to know the rest of the story.

"My father is Uranus," said Aphrodite, patting her arm. "But that is a story for another time."

Was Aphrodite admitting she was a Titan, and only an honorary Olympian? More curiously, was she expecting to see Amphitrite again, so she could tell her the story of her birth? Amphitrite was desperate to know, but they reached the rose garden and so she pressed her lips shut.

"Ah, here we are," said Aphrodite, releasing Amphitrite's arm to inspect a particularly large red rose in full bloom. "Aren't they lovely?"

Amphitrite followed, leaning over to get a closer look at the flower. She clasped her hands together as she examined it, to stop herself from reaching out and touching it. They didn't have such things in the sea. The closest was anemone, but they stung when touched. These flowers looked like they were made to be caressed, and Amphitrite wondered if its petals felt as velvety as they looked.

Aphrodite laughed, having seen Amphitrite's mouth drop open with curiosity and then purse tight with restraint.

"I see the way Poseidon looks at you," said Aphrodite, plucking a stem from the climbing bush before them and bringing it to her nose. She closed her eyes in pure bliss, breathing in the flower's fragrance. After, she held it out to Amphitrite for a sniff. "I know it well. He will do anything for you."

Amphitrite wanted clarification on the bold statement, but instead, she leaned forward and inhaled deeply. She was still learning how to interact with the unpredictable gods and goddesses of Olympus. So far, she hadn't roused any of their ire, and she did not want to start now.

The heady scent was unlike anything else she had experienced. It filled her with a warmth she could not describe. It wasn't a physical reaction, but more a feeling of deep appreciation for Gaia and all the beautiful things she'd created for the land dwellers, just as Oceanus had created so many beguiling things for the sea folk.

"Are you lovers?" Amphitrite blurted out the question, suddenly needing to know. "You and Poseidon, I mean." It was a fair question, and one that needed to be answered. She'd seen Aphrodite and Poseidon talking in hushed tones earlier. It made Amphitrite think back to the night she was chosen.

She could not bear it if she must enter yet another competition for Poseidon's favor.

Aphrodite sighed, as though she knew this question would be asked and did not care to answer. "No, but I will not lie and say we never have been."

"Oh…" Amphitrite gripped the rose tighter, gasping when the sharp tip of a thorn sank into her finger. A reminder that something so beautiful could bring both pleasure and pain.

"You have nothing to fear, Amphitrite," replied Aphrodite, taking the rose back and carefully snapping the thorns off the stem. "Our passion for each other burned out long ago. The only thing that consumes us now is friendship."

Aphrodite tucked the rose into the hair behind Amphitrite's ear. "He is taken with another."

"Me," whispered Amphitrite, watching the tiny bead of blood rise on the tip of her finger. "How am I to know it is not lust that drives him?"

"If that were the case, you would not be here now." Aphrodite took her finger, swiping her thumb over the tiny prick mark. "He would have forced his will upon you already. And he most certainly would never have sent Delphin on his behalf to beg for your return. He has shown much restraint, and it is because he cares for you."

The small wound disappeared, as if it had never existed. Amphitrite bit her lip. Aphrodite was persuasive, there was no denying that. But did she speak the truth?

"He is difficult at times, yes, but there is a reason," continued Aphrodite. "Poseidon is as proud as he is passionate. When he was swallowed by his father..."

Amphitrite winced, unable to fathom something so terrible and tragic.

"He was only a child and could not save himself, and so there he stayed, growing older in the dark with his siblings. They were alone, and he grew furious at their helpless situation, but, of course, his rage was impotent. No matter how much he thrashed about, pounding on the walls of their terrible prison, they were trapped. Can you imagine it? No way out... Well, that is until Zeus came to their rescue. Poseidon was filled with gratitude when they were saved, to be sure, but his younger brother's fame soon began to plague him. As you know, fame is everything to the gods."

"He feels pale in comparison to Zeus," said Amphitrite, putting the pieces together. Aphrodite did speak truth, and as she was learning, the goddess had the same altruistic heart that Amphitrite herself possessed. "He overreacts because he feels weak."

"Yes, and it was only I who understood this about him... until now."

CHAPTER 22

Amphitrite heard all she needed to hear, but when the goddess looked into her eyes, reaching out and brushing her fingertips along the place where Amphitrite's heart beat in her chest, she knew for certain.

She would be Poseidon's queen.

Aphrodite smiled meaningfully at her. "It won't always be easy, but you will love and be loved for an immortal lifetime, my darling."

Amphitrite's limbs tingled, her head feeling light as air as she nodded.

"I know what you say is true." She was overcome with a feeling of affection for Poseidon as she said it. "Fate has brought us together, but it is love that will keep us from parting. And I do…"

"What, my darling?" The Goddess of Love waited for her answer with a satisfied smile edging the corners of her mouth upwards.

The tests were done, and Amphitrite could not wait one moment longer to speak her truth, shouting it from the top of the highest mountain. She must return to the great hall, as fast as her feet could carry her, and tell her love the good news he'd been waiting so patiently for.

She loved him, like Tethys loved Oceanus. Fully, passionately, and unconditionally.

"That I love him," replied Amphitrite. "Let us go back. I've waited long enough. I must confess my intent to him now."

The admission left her chest heaving and her lungs breathless. Her heart flitted in her ribcage like butterfly wings as they turned to make their way back to the great hall of the Olympians' polished and gleaming marble palace.

"Yes, of course." Aphrodite threaded her arm around Amphitrite's waist as they rushed down the stone path.

One moment they were surrounded by shrubs and hedges of the garden labyrinth, the next they were in the great hall, rushing toward Poseidon, who sat on a cushioned chair as he conversed with Zeus. She stumbled, dizzied and disoriented from the sudden change in scenery, but quickly regained her balance. She blinked the scene into focus, vaguely aware Delphin was there, too, but she kept her eyes fixed on her soon-to-be husband.

Poseidon stopped talking, his brows angling downward at the sight of her. And what a sight she must be; flustered, sweating, and stumbling toward him. If not for Aphrodite's guidance, Amphitrite very well might have tripped over her own two feet.

Poseidon stood, his chair sliding back noisily, almost tipping over with the force and speed with which he rose to his feet.

"Amphitrite? What's wrong?" He rushed over, taking her by both shoulders and inspecting her before cutting his gaze to Aphrodite. "What happened?"

Aphrodite laughed breezily. "Love, you fool." She tilted her head at Poseidon, unbothered by his sternness. "Amphitrite has something she would like to tell you. What was it you said, darling? A confession?" The goddess set her sparkling gaze on Amphitrite, arching an eyebrow. "I believe it is more of a conviction, but go ahead, tell him what you told me."

Amphitrite glanced around the great hall. Zeus stared at her with a raised eyebrow and a knowing smirk. Hera looked on from her throne with barely contained interest. Hebe, who'd been filling their cups, was biting her bottom lip and looking as though she were ready to burst with excitement. They all seemed elated. Except Athena, who loomed in the distance looking thoroughly disinterested.

"I will be your queen," she said proudly, not caring whether any of them approved or disapproved.

Poseidon inhaled sharply.

"Amphitrite, my love." Poseidon raised his voice as he, too, glanced around the room. "And I say that here and now, in front of all because I do love her." His gaze returned to hers. "There is nothing I wanted to hear you say more, but…" His green eyes filled with emotion as he cupped her face with his hands. "I don't want you to be my wife because you feel sorry for me, or you're afraid, or as some selfless way to protect your family." He glanced at Aphrodite. "Or because you have been convinced with sweet talk." He looked into Amphitrite's eyes again, his brows raising earnestly. "I want you to marry me because you love me."

Amphitrite's heart cracked wide open, releasing all the fear and doubt she'd kept trapped inside her for far too long.

"I am marrying you because I love you," replied Amphitrite.

That was all it took for the Olympians to break out in a round of cheers and applause.

"Ha! Did you hear that? She's agreed to marry him!" cried Zeus, throwing his arms wide. "Oh, sweet and gentle Hebe, bring us more wine!"

Hermes flew over on winged feet, wrapping Amphitrite in a warm embrace. "Welcome to the family," he said before turning toward Poseidon. "If you ever need someone to look after those fine white horses of yours..." Hermes clapped Poseidon on the back, his smile widening at the same time Poseidon's gaze narrowed. "Oh, come now, King of the Sea, I jest. Congratulations. Fate has finally smiled down upon you."

CHAPTER 23

Poseidon stroked the soft waves of Amphitrite's hair as they lay on the shore watching the last vestiges of a spectacular sunset sink beneath the waves. They were to be married the next morning, here on this beach, standing in the surf so they could be both on land and in the sea as they said their vows.

The announcement had been well received, with the bellows of Zeus's approval still ringing in Poseidon's ears. He and Amphitrite had drunk to their health, beaming at the shouts of congratulations. He, too, had sloshed a good amount of wine before noticing how raucous the Olympians were becoming, especially Ares. He could tell it overwhelmed his bride-to-be, and so he'd taken her hand and led her down to the shore where they could be alone.

Holding her in his arms there, where the sea met land, felt right. True, they were filthy and covered in sand, but the sound of the waves crashing against the shore soothed them both, and neither cared a wit about what was happening in the great hall, so long as they were alone.

Lying with her tucked safely in his arms, he could hardly wait for them to be back at his golden palace. He had half a mind to drag the Olympians away from whatever debauchery they were currently engaging in so they could be joined that very moment.

"Will Delphin be there?" murmured Amphitrite, content in tracing the dips and ridges of his shoulder instead of getting rip roaring drunk. And he was content to let her. "I didn't see him after the announcement."

"No," replied Poseidon, musing how neatly she fit into the crook of his arm. The thought led him to wonder if their bodies would fit just as perfectly. For now, he would simply hold her close, but he longed for the time when Amphitrite's passion finally ignited.

"Why not?" She went up on one elbow to look at him. "He is the reason we are to be married tomorrow morning, in front of Zeus and the others, is it not?"

"He is," said Poseidon, taking the hand she had laid on his chest and kissing the back of it. "But he will not be here because he is there." He nodded up at the night sky.

Amphitrite let out a small gasp. "Up there, among the stars?"

"It is a great honor, Amphitrite," he replied. "One he accepted freely and without haste."

Neither of them spoke as they gazed up at the newly formed constellation in the night sky. Poseidon grinned, thinking fondly of how the smile had practically cracked the old sea daemon's face in half right before he'd sent him to his place of honor among the stars.

"I suppose he was growing older." Amphitrite sighed before nestling deeper into his side. "Now he can live on forever. Just like our love. I shall miss him, though."

"Indeed," replied Poseidon.

He would miss his faithful old friend, without whom he would not have Amphitrite in his arms at long last. It was because of the old sea daemon they would be bound as husband and wife by the law of the gods; something which he wanted more than immortal life itself. However, it would be untrue to say their impending nuptials didn't make him nervous.

Forever was a long time to control the violence and destruction that, until now, had free reign.

"What did you say to Galatea?" she asked lightly.

It seemed she was satisfied with the fate of Delphin, but the question about her sister surprised him, pushing his worries of self-control—or lack thereof—aside, at least for the time being.

"I told her that if she was truly in love with the mortal, she should not waste a chance at happiness so graciously given to her by The Fates."

"I hope she does," she said, sounding wistful. "Marry him, that is. Do you think he will ask her to?"

"Even if he does, I don't think Doris will allow it," he sighed. "In hindsight, I believe the only reason she suggested Galatea was to prevent the tryst from going any further."

"But you could command her to allow it," she said, sliding an arm over his chest, her fingers trailing along his side. A moment later her caresses suddenly stopped. "Wait... *I* could command her to allow it."

He cleared his throat, loosening the words that had become stuck. It wasn't his intention to change the direction of the conversation, but his anxious thoughts persisted, making it hard to think of anything else. If they were to be together for the rest of time, he must take his own advice. He must divulge his worries to her, so they could face them together.

"Amphitrite," he said, feeling her body go rigid.

"I didn't... I didn't mean to sound..." she stammered.

"No, my love, you didn't sound cruel. Come here." He pulled her on top of him, cupping her face so that he could look her in the eyes. "You will be my queen, with the power to rule over the sea alongside me. If that is the price your mother pays for her prejudice, then you have my support." He brushed a thumb over her cheek lightly as he searched for what to say next. Delicacy was needed, which was not exactly his strong suit. "What I mean to say is that I love you more than I thought possible, and although I am an Olympian, I am..." He couldn't believe what he was about to confess. "I am not perfect. I will always love and respect *you*, but I cannot promise my anger will never rise against others. This worries me. I'm at peace with you by my side, but you cannot always be there with me."

"No, but I can be in your mind and in your heart. A promise that our kingdom does not suffer the consequences of your anger, this is all I can ask of you."

"The innocents of the sea will not be harmed. You have my word. And I shall never raise a hand to you... or our children."

She relaxed at the mention of a family of their own, sighing deeply.

"I believe you" she replied before pressing her lips to his. Afterward, she laid her head on his chest, surrendering her own fears. "Come what may, we will face it together."

With his fellow gods and goddesses looking on, Poseidon handed Amphitrite her trident. It fit in her hand perfectly. Her smile was so radiant it outshined the elaborate crown of glittering jewels—and barnacles—resting atop her precious head. They'd said their vows, and it was time to seal them with a kiss.

He leaned down, his kiss slow and sensual despite having an audience. He sought to give her a taste of what pleasure was to come later that evening. Perhaps even as soon as they were back at their golden palace beneath the waves.

She reached up, sliding her fingers into his hair and pulling him closer, deepening the kiss to indicate she looked forward to whatever he had in store for her.

They continued reveling in each other until he could no longer ignore the way the waves crashed against their ankles insistently, beckoning them to return to the sea where they belonged.

"Ready?" he said, lifting his trident.

Gold glinting in the sunlight, Amphitrite lifted hers in return. "Ready."

Determined to be the god she deserved, he smiled at her adoringly as they tapped the ends of their matching tridents on the rocky ground in unison, leaving the land behind to rule their kingdom beneath the waves.

THE END

GET A PREVIEW OF THE PRINCESS AND THE PROPHECY

Cassandra smiled as she pulled back the string of her bow and aimed the tip of an arrow at a tree. It wasn't customary for women to learn archery, but she was a princess, the daughter of King Priam and Queen Hecuba of Troy, and so she was allowed to bend the rules, especially on her eighteenth name day.

The bow, crafted of sturdy maple and coveted by many a soldier in the Trojan army, had been a gift. Cassandra was accustomed to receiving such fine things from her father's people, but the bow had not been from just anyone.

"Steady now," called out the man standing next to the tree. "Close one eye if you must." The man was striking in appearance, tall and lean-muscled, with burnished curls that shined brightly, even in the dim light of the forest.

It was no wonder they did. He who stood before her was no man, but Apollo, the God of Sun and Light, holding domain over many things, including archery. The bow had been his gift to Cassandra on her sixteenth name day.

Determined to keep both eyes open this time, she zeroed in on a particularly large knot in the bark and let loose her arrow. It pierced through the rough outer layer and sunk deep into the heart of the tree. She lowered her bow, sending Apollo a triumphant grin.

"A fluke," he teased, shaking his head in amusement at her capricious nature as he pulled the arrow out as easily as though he were plucking fruit.

Cassandra's heart danced in her chest, her cheeks warming at the display of raw power. Oh, what she wouldn't give to possess some of it. Alas, she had not been born a goddess, and suspected the reason the god of music and dancing and poetry favored her was for her beauty, certainly, but more importantly, her cleverness.

"Perhaps I shall go again," shouted Cassandra, "to prove you wrong." She withdrew another arrow from the quiver strapped to her back. She felt brave enough to cajole the god in this way. He'd been visiting her for two years, after all.

Though many months had passed, she remembered their first encounter like it was the day before. It had been a lovely morning, much like this one, sunny and mild, with a slight breeze to lift the ends of her dark mahogany hair. She and her twin brother, Helenus, had been practicing shooting arrows at this very spot. After a few hours, her brother had gone in search of bread and cheese to fill his growling belly, but Cassandra had stayed behind, shooting her arrows until blisters formed on her fingers. She had always been headstrong, and she was determined to surpass her brother's naturally good marksmanship.

Now, she nocked an arrow on the very same bow Apollo had given her that day, ready to take aim, when a vision of Helenus approaching from behind flashed in her mind's eye. On her seventeenth name day, Apollo had given her the gift of foresight. Thanks to her, Helenus had received it as well.

"I see your aim has gotten better," her brother shouted from afar.

She lowered her bow at the sound of his voice, whirling around and pretending to be startled.

Helenus chuckled. "There is no need for show, sister. Not with our minds. How do you think I knew you would be here? Besides, I was noisier than a wild boar barging through the brush."

"It was not a difficult thing to know," she replied, a bit indignant. She loved Helenus dearly, but things had always come easy to him. He'd been born a boy, affording him more liberties than her from the moment they left the womb. It irked her at times like this, when he patronized. "I always come here on our name day."

What she did not say aloud was she always came on this day, to this spot, to receive whatever gift Apollo would bestow upon her. He would appear at other times, of course, but meeting here on her name day had become a tradition, so he could give her a gift. It had been the bow first, followed by foresight the next year. She was anxious to know what her eighteenth name day gift would be.

Some days she wondered if she should have kept the foresight to herself instead of sharing it. She'd agreed to accept it on the condition that her twin would receive the same. She didn't know why she'd done it, but it wasn't for Helenus's sake, that much she knew. She supposed she'd done it to see how far Apollo would go, and exactly how much of his divine power she could talk him into giving her.

But, at times like this, when Helenus made it difficult to ever be alone, she regretted it.

Cassandra glanced back at the tree where Apollo had been standing. The arrow stuck out of its thick trunk, but, as always when anyone else approached unexpectedly, the god had vanished. Apollo only showed himself to her, which was an honor she cherished, but it made her behavior seem rather strange to the others, even Helenus at times. For all the foresight he possessed, he had no idea it was because *she* was favored by Apollo.

As close as they were, she didn't think Helenus could suspend such disbelief. She'd tried broaching the subject once, and although he agreed their gift was divine, he refused to acknowledge that it had been bestowed upon them because his sister had caught the eye of the God of Prophecy himself. He or her parents, and sometimes her maid, would often see her talking to herself, but they could not fathom she could be conversing with the divine.

She had tried to explain this many times, that she was favored by one of the very gods who built their city's impenetrable walls, but they all chose to believe she simply had the wildest of imaginations. This seemed strange to Cassandra, especially given that her own mother was said to sometimes have prophetic dreams.

"It's a good thing archers rely on their eyes and not their ears, dear brother," replied Cassandra, dismissing the thought and hoping her remark was enough of a segue. "What brings you out here to interrupt my practice?"

The smile dropped from his face. She hated when her brother went serious like this. It meant only one thing.

"I've come to ask if you've seen him," he replied.

Cassandra swallowed hard, knowing the man her brother spoke of. The shepherd. The one on his way to the festival their father hosted each year. The one who looked so much like their older brother Hector that they, too, could be twins.

"Yes," she said, barely audible. Suddenly, her eyes glazed as a vision overtook her mind. The way the shepherd laughed with his traveling companions, free and easy and heartily. Though it didn't happen as often now that he had grown older, this was the way their father laughed.

Without warning, the vision of the young man switched to their mother, sweaty from labor. She cried as she held a newborn baby, but they were not tears of joy. Anguish crumpled her features as she stroked a shock of dark hair before a nursemaid whisked the baby away.

Cassandra blinked away both the tears and the vision. One look at Helenus's wide eyes and furrowed brow and she knew he'd seen it, too. She and Helenus had heard the stories whispered among the palace maids of a stillborn baby who had come only a few years before her and Helenus's birth, and how Hecuba did not leave her chambers for months.

"He lives," she whispered. "Our brother lives."

The Author

Forever a fan of fairytales, folklore, and mythology, Kerri brings life to the mythological characters you know and love... or love to hate.

Kerri lives in Michigan with her husband, son and cat they lovingly but aptly refer to as The Maleficence. Mel for short. If Kerri isn't raking leaves or shoveling snow, she's either reading, writing or has fled her evil to-do list and fallen down an Internet rabbit hole... Or possibly just fallen and can't get up.

For news and updates about upcoming releases, sign up for Kerri's newsletter at kerrikeberly.com. For an inside look at the day in the life of a crafty crochet-addicted, DIY-loving, Greek mythology-obsessed author, follow her on Facebook, Instagram, and TikTok.